SOME SECRETS ARE JUST TOO GOOD TO KEEP TO YOURSELF!

Sugar Secrets...
1 ... & Revenge
2 ... & Rivals
3 ... & Lies
4 ... & Freedom
5 ... & Lust
6 ... & Mistakes
7 ... & Choices
8 ... & Ambition

Sugar
SECRETS...

...& Lust

Mel Sparke

Collins

An imprint of HarperCollins*Publishers*

Published in Great Britain by Collins in 1999
Collins is an imprint of HarperCollins*Publishers* Ltd
77–85 Fulham Palace Road, Hammersmith, London W6 8JB

The HarperCollins website address is
www.fireandwater.com

9 8 7 6 5 4 3 2 1

Creative consultant: Sue Dando
Copyright © Sugar 1999. Licensed with TLC.

ISBN 0 00 675443 0

Printed and bound in Great Britain by
Caledonian International Book Manufacturing Ltd, Glasgow

CHAPTER 1

• •

GIRLS' NIGHT IN

"Oh my God, I look like Lily Savage!" Sonja Harvey stared at her reflection in the mirror with horror.

"Don't exaggerate. You look sophisticated, sort of classy, like a Hollywood film star." Catrina Osgood was delighted with the new look she'd just given her cousin.

"More like a Hollywood hooker, I'd say. I can't believe you've done this to me, Cat..."

"Oh, come on, Son, you're over-reacting! If I'd thought you were going to make this much fuss, I would never have offered to do it in the first place."

"*Offer*? It was hardly an offer. You practically frogmarched me in here! All I did was happen to mention that I fancied a make-over and you'd got

5

me in here before I had time to finish the sentence. And now look at me!" Sonja pulled a face at her own reflection. "The foundation's so thick it looks like you've put it on with a trowel. There's glitter on my chin, and eyeshadow on my temples and in my hair." Unable to bear looking at her unrecognisable self any longer, she glared at Cat. "Are you *blind* or something?"

"It's *supposed* to be like that, you idiot. It's my Disco Queen look, for when you're in a dark club. It's meant to bring your features out when the light's not so good. Honestly, Sonja, I can't believe you're so unwilling to try something new. If you ever decide to take up modelling, you'll have to be a bit more adventurous with your looks, you know."

Sonja flinched. She'd toyed with the idea of modelling in the past, but she'd never really decided whether it was going to be a serious option or not.

"Let's get the others." Cat headed for the door. "I bet they'll love it and you'll wonder what you were making such a fuss about."

Sonja couldn't bear the thought of her friends seeing her like this.

"You must be joking! I'm not leaving this bedroom until all this muck is off my face. Pass me my cleanser, will you?"

But it was too late. Catrina had opened the bedroom door. She scurried eagerly on to the Harveys' landing and called downstairs to the living room where Kerry was giving Maya a manicure.

"Come on, girls! I've finished. Sonja's transformation is complete. And fantastic, if I say so myself."

Kerry Bellamy stopped buffing Maya's right index finger, looked at her friend and rolled her eyes dramatically.

"This I've *got* to see," she said, getting up off the floor and heading for the stairs. Maya followed, a look of trepidation on her face.

These girlie get-togethers at Sonja's house (no one else had enough space) were a laugh, but Cat's bossy enthusiasm and tendency to hijack the proceedings often grated on Kerry. She had been relieved when Cat had picked Sonja to be make-over guinea pig for the night and dreaded to think what a beauty-product addict like Cat had done to their effortlessly gorgeous friend.

Sonja was still in her room, frantically turning her dressing table upside-down in a fruitless search for her cleanser. Then Catrina came back into the room, waving a bottle in her hand.

"Looking for this?" she grinned.

"You cow...!"

"Aw, come on, you're not destroying all my hard work that easily."

At that moment, Kerry and Maya walked in and gasped in unison.

"Fabulous, isn't it?" beamed Catrina.

Maya stared wide-eyed at Sonja's face and struggled to find something positive to say. It was difficult, since Maya thought her friend looked ridiculous.

For once, Kerry wasn't so reticent.

"It's Eddie Izzard," she laughed. Then, seeing the thunderous look on Sonja's face, she swiftly changed tack. "Uhhh, only joking, Son. It's just a bit of a shock to see you in any make-up at all. You look, er, different, sort of older. More mature. Anyway, it's certainly eye-catching..."

"Yeah," added Maya, "it's interesting. Very daring..."

"And totally gross," Sonja grimaced. She pointed a finger at her cousin. "I can't believe I was daft enough to let *her* loose on my face like that. No wonder she wouldn't let me see until it was finished. She just wanted to make a fool of me."

Catrina's smile vanished and she glared furiously at Sonja. "I can*not* believe you think that. I was only trying to do something different. I won't bother next time."

Sensing that things were beginning to get out of hand, Maya tried to diffuse the situation.

"To be honest, I think you're both being a little over-sensitive here. Everyone has different styles and ideas when it comes to putting on make-up. It's just that both of yours are worlds apart. What's so bad about that?"

Kerry nodded vigorously, encouraging Maya to go on.

"Catrina would look great made up like that, Son," continued Maya, "and I think it's, er, really nice of her to try it on you. Even if you've decided that it isn't right for you. At least now you know."

"I bet if you turned the tables and tried out one of your unmade-up make-up looks on Cat, she wouldn't be so keen on it either," put in Kerry. "And then you'd be really offended, wouldn't you?"

Sonja nodded grudgingly.

"What I'm saying," Maya carried on, "is that the whole point of these girls' nights in is for us all to try out new things, have a laugh and a bit of fun."

She sat down on the bed. "I mean, one of the things I'd love to do tonight is try on that new pink top of yours, Son. Not because I think I'll look great in it, but to confirm that it's totally wrong for me. Once I know that, I won't need to

humiliate myself in front of a load of Miss Selfridge shop assistants by trying one on and looking stupid in it. You guys will be doing me a favour by telling me instead."

Suitably distracted, Sonja went to her wardrobe and pulled the candy-coloured top from its hanger.

"Is this the one you mean?"

"Yeah." Maya took the top and began rubbing the material between her fingers. "It's *gorgeous*. I keep having fantasies about being able to wear something like this. But I know it's totally the wrong colour and style for me. I just need to try it on to break the fantasy."

"Go on then," said Sonja. "I bet it'll look great on you."

Maya pulled off the sloppy T-shirt she was wearing and hauled the stretchy material over her head. Adjusting herself in the mirror she turned resignedly to her friends and shrugged.

"See? Dreadful. Total failure. Clothes like these should come with a health warning saying that Maya Joshi or anyone else not built like Kate Moss should avoid them at all costs. Am I right?"

Sonja scratched her head and frowned. "Uh, yeah. I guess you are."

"Just like I didn't realise quite how much you'd hate that make-up," Catrina added.

"Yeah, maybe you're right."

The doorbell rang.

"Oh, fab, pizza's here," cried Kerry and rushed out of the room, followed by Maya. "Come on, everyone, *Titanic*'s ready to go on the video. The tissues are on standby. Let's eat!" she yelled back over her shoulder as she ran down the stairs.

"I won't be a tick," Sonja said. "I'll just, er, clean up my face, then I'll be down. Thanks for the make-over, Cat," she added as she headed for the bathroom. "And sorry I was so ungrateful. It was just a bit of a shock."

"No worries. Maybe I'll try out my Beach Babe look on you next time," said Cat with a grin.

CHAPTER 2

●●●●●●●●●●●●●●●●●●●●●●●●●●●●

CAT'S CHALLENGE

"Hurry up and...(*sniff*) pass the tissues please, Son (*sniff*). My glasses are all steamed up."

"Sorry, Kez. Didn't mean to hog them. It's j-j-just that this film is *sooo* sad."

"I know. I can't believe I've seen it about twenty times and it still makes me cry..."

"I know. And Leonardo DiCaprio is *sooo* cute. He doesn't deserve to die."

"But it wouldn't be such a good film if he'd lived, would it?" Maya began analysing as the end credits to *Titanic* rolled in front of them on the TV screen. "I mean, it's only so blubworthy *because* he dies. Otherwise, it'd be like any other love story with a run of the mill perfect ending."

"Yeah, Maya's right," Catrina added. "It wouldn't be half as good if they all lived happily

ever after. Anyway, I'm glad he dies. He looks like a nasty little rodent with those beady eyes and tiny mouth. I can't see what all the fuss is about him being such a hunk. I've seen better-looking guys than him at St Mark's. *Arrrgh!*"

Catrina squealed and ducked to avoid the cushions that Sonja and Kerry had hurled at her.

"How can you say that?" wailed Sonja. "I'll tell you, if there was a guy even half as good-looking as him at college, then I'd be going out with him by now."

"Me too," Maya added.

"As it is," Sonja went on, "Kerry's got the only decent boyfriend around here, while the rest of us sit around wondering if we're going to end up like a bunch of sad old spinsters."

"Speak for yourself," said Catrina archly. "I'll have you know I've got guys falling over themselves trying to go out with me at the moment. I don't think I've ever been so popular."

"So what are you doing here with us on a Saturday night then?" Sonja asked. "Why aren't you snogging the face off some poor victim somewhere?"

"Well, a girl's got to have the odd night off, you know. If I didn't, I'd be worn out."

"Anyway," added Maya, "I don't know what you're complaining about, Sonja Harvey. You

must get more offers than the rest of us put together."

"Pah, don't you believe it!" Sonja snorted indignantly. "I can't remember the last time I had an offer from anyone other than one of the two-headed, single-brain-celled monsters round here. It's so long since I had a snog, I've almost forgotten where my lips are."

"Well, at least you're getting interest," Maya continued, "however unwelcome it might be. It must boost your ego to know someone fancies you, even if you don't like them back. I'd be flattered if I knew anyone was after me..."

"Not if he was a complete idiot, you wouldn't," giggled Sonja. "And I don't know what you're moaning about, Maya. That Billy from your photography club is desperate to go out with you."

"It's not like that. He's just a friend."

"But only by your choosing. If I remember rightly – and I do – you had the hots for him at first. Then you had one date with the poor guy and suddenly you cooled off."

Maya looked perplexed. Sonja was right. She could have started going out with Billy, but something had made her back off before they'd even got to the holding hands stage. At first she'd thought it was because she sensed (wrongly, as it turned out) that *he* was more interested in the

fact that Maya was Asian than *she* was. She soon realised it was more than that though.

"I know," she muttered. "I just decided we'd get along better as friends. I can't tell you why exactly. It was a gut feeling. But before I met Billy there was no one, and there's nobody new on the horizon."

"The problem with you guys is you're far too picky," Catrina said, and looked genuinely surprised when the others fell about laughing.

"Unlike you, you mean," Sonja finally managed to say between giggles.

"Actually, no, I didn't mean that at all," Catrina shot back. "But it's like this. I think that you should try all the cakes in the shop in order to find the one that you like best. I mean, some guys are like jam doughnuts – nothing special to look at but totally delish when you take that first bite." She paused. "You haven't got anything else to eat have you, Son? I'm still starving and that pizza was so tiny."

"Only bourbons," said Sonja, heading for the kitchen to raid the biscuit tin. "Anyway, there is this one guy that I might be interested in..."

She left the room to uniform yells of "Who?! Quick, tell us!"

"*Wee-lll*," she carried on as she came back with two family packs of chocolate biscuits, "he's

not in the same league as Leonardo, not even in the same stratosphere, but I reckon he's the best I've seen for a while. Above average for a Winstead lad, anyway..." Her voice tailed off to a tantalising silence.

"So?!" wailed Kerry. "Come on, Son, what else? What's his name? Do we know him? What's he look like? Does he know you? Have you spoken to him? Spill the beans!"

Sonja laughed. "I knew that piece of news would get you going. His name is Kyle. I remember him from a couple of years back when he had a summer job alongside Lottie at the superstore. I never paid him much attention until last week when I saw him working in that new sports shop in the Plaza with a whole new haircut. Total transformation – amazingly cute. You wouldn't think it was the same guy."

"Oh, yeah, I think I vaguely remember him," Kerry butted in excitedly.

"Anyway, he definitely saw me gawping at him in the street because he smiled and sort of mouthed hello really cheekily, but that's as far as it's gone to date. I really can't tell you anything more."

"Come on, you must!" howled Catrina. "I mean, you said he's cute. How cute? Who does he look like – anyone famous? Are you besotted,

or just mildly interested because there's no one else on the scene and you're desperate? Come *on*, Son, what's the story?"

Sonja ran her fingers through her honey-blonde hair and sighed dramatically.

"I am *not* desperate," she stressed, "and I'm not besotted either. But he is kind of the only guy who's raised my heartbeat even a little bit in the last few months. And there's something about him that reminds me of David Beckham, now he's got the haircut..."

"So what are you going to do about it? Have you got a plan of action?" Catrina demanded. "'Ten ways to get him to notice you', that kind of thing?"

"I haven't thought about it that much," shrugged Sonja, even though she had really. "I'll probably wait and see what develops."

"Ooh, you mustn't do that," Catrina chided. "You need to have a plan. I always do, even if I know he's a sure thing. You need to have a whole bunch of opening lines, to get the conversation rolling. And I always know within the first five minutes whether a guy's interested in me or not, just by watching his reactions."

"What do you mean – if he doesn't throw up, there's a chance he might fancy you?" Sonja grinned mischievously.

"Ha ha! What I'm saying is that if he seems to be listening intently to me, and if he keeps his eyes on mine, there's a good chance he's interested. But if he keeps looking over my shoulder, or if he's giving one-word answers, or has his arms folded across his chest *defensively*, then I'm probably wasting my time."

"I read in a magazine that it's a good sign if the guy you're interested in starts to mimic your actions," said Maya. "So if you take a sip of your drink, he copies, or if you stand with your elbow on the bar, he does the same."

Kerry looked somewhat bewildered by all of this. She'd never heard anything so contrived in all her life. She certainly couldn't ever remember being that calculating when she started to fancy Ollie. It all seemed to happen much more naturally than that.

"The thing you lot seem to be forgetting," she ventured finally, "is that Sonja doesn't need any of these tips on how to score. She only has to smile at a guy to get him to fall for her. I've seen it happen loads of times."

"Aw, you say the nicest things!" Sonja smiled sweetly at Kerry. "And the best thing is, it's all absolutely true. As soon as Kyle realises I'm on to him, he won't know what's hit him."

Catrina shot her cousin a scathing look. "You

are confident," she said, a challenging note in her voice.

"Yeah, reasonably," answered Sonja.

"OK, why don't we see just how good your pulling power is?"

"What do you mean?"

"Well," Catrina said, thinking out loud, "if you're so sure this Kyle guy will fall for you, you won't mind if I give you a deadline to work towards."

"What sort of deadline?"

"Well, how about I give you a week to get him to go out with you?"

"Easy." Sonja smiled even more confidently, then added, "Assuming, of course, that I actually see him in the next seven days."

"Of course."

"OK then. You're on!"

CHAPTER 3

•

SONJA SOUNDS OFF

Kerry sat on the edge of the spare bed in Sonja's room in her pyjamas working moisturiser into her face with her fingers. She was pleased to be staying the night; it had been a while since the last Sonja'n'Kerry sleepover and it was great to have a chance to catch up.

But the fact that Sonja hadn't mentioned anything about fancying a guy before now surprised Kerry slightly: there would have been a time when she'd have been the first to know. After all, Sonja had been the first person to suss out Kerry's love for Ollie and had then cajoled her friend into revealing her feelings.

In fact, it was Sonja's probing questions that had made Kerry realise just how deeply she felt about Ollie.

Now that the other two had gone home Kerry felt able to tackle her about the subject.

"So why didn't you tell me about Kyle before?"

"Sorry?" Sonja turned from where she was sitting at her dressing table and gave Kerry a quizzical look. "What do you mean?"

"Well, I just thought that if you were into someone new, *normally* you would have been on the phone to me straightaway. Filling me in on all the gory details."

"I know, but..." Sonja stopped short of telling Kerry why she hadn't confided in her before. The fact that Kerry had become so involved with Ollie since they'd started going out – almost to the exclusion of everything else – had really begun to bother her. Even when the gang were together, Sonja sensed that Ollie and Kerry were very much a couple rather than part of the crowd.

And yet she knew how sensitive her friend could be and wasn't sure her thoughts were worth bringing out into the open just yet, if at all.

"But what?"

Still Sonja didn't answer. She walked round to her bed, slid under the duvet and hugged her knees. Kerry watched her movements, a furrow of concern etched on her face.

"Come on, Son," she persisted. "Tell me. It's obvious that something's bugging you."

"OK, OK, I will. But promise me you won't get upset?"

"Uh, sure. No, of course I won't," Kerry answered, suddenly very anxious.

"Well, you're right. Normally I would have been on the phone to you or called in at your house to tell you all about Kyle. But the thing is, Kez, you've been so wrapped up in Ollie recently that I haven't been able to spend much time with you, let alone get down to the nitty-gritty of what's been going on in my life."

Kerry raised her eyebrows and opened her mouth as if to protest.

"And before you object," Sonja carried on, "that isn't a criticism as such, because I think it's great what you and Ollie have got together, I really do. It's just that when you're not actually *with* Ollie or doing your summer job at the chemist's, then you're on the phone to him or hanging out at the café or at Nick's Slick Riffs, depending on where he's working."

Sonja took a deep breath and sighed. "I guess I just feel a bit neglected, that's all."

Kerry felt as if she was about to cry. Of course, it was all true – she simply hadn't seen it before. Having Sonja sit there and spell it out to her made her feel totally wretched.

She was, it had to be said, completely besotted

with Ollie. She'd never had a boyfriend before and to be going out with such a warm-hearted, gorgeous, loving, thoughtful person as Ollie had completely blown her away. She ate, slept and dreamt Ollie Stanton.

Now, when she thought about it, Kerry realised that she hadn't been out with Sonja – *just* Sonja – for ages; the truth was, she couldn't even remember the last time. Sure, they saw each other at the café with the rest of the gang, but more often than not Ollie was there too. And Sonja was right – Kerry's attention was always mainly on him.

She had even thought about crying off this girls' night in, not because she could have gone out with Ollie instead – he was seeing Joe – but because she would have preferred a night in on her own, watching TV and drifting off into warm, cosy thoughts about her boyfriend. In the end, Kerry'd really had to force herself to come along.

What a cow! she thought. *No wonder Sonja's hacked off with me.*

Kerry groped around on the bed for her wire-framed glasses and hastily put them back on so she could see Sonja's face.

"Son, I'm so sorry," she wailed, looking earnestly at her friend. "You're absolutely right – I've been selfish. I've been so head over heels in

love with Ollie that I've thought of little else for weeks. You must hate me!"

Sonja shook her head and smiled. "No, not at all. Despaired of you a little, maybe, but of course I don't hate you. And I don't begrudge what you and Ollie have. It must be wonderful to be so in love with someone and to know that they're equally into you. But I would hate us to drift apart. I reckon that would be a big mistake."

"I know. Talk about love is blind and all that. Oh, God! I must have seemed really pathetic, all loved-up and gooey-eyed. It must have been nauseating for you. And the others. Has anyone else said anything?"

"Nope. Not a word. Well, only nice stuff. Honestly, Kez, it's not a big deal. I wasn't even going to mention it until you kept on at me. But now that it's out in the open, it's up to you to decide what you do about it. If anything. Like I said, it's not a big problem."

Sonja snuggled down under her duvet and closed her eyes, totally relaxed.

"If you're sure. Thanks for being so understanding, Son," said Kerry, climbing into her bed and taking her glasses off again. "Hey, to make amends, let's have a night out together. And I promise I won't waffle on about Ollie! I won't even mention his name."

"Don't be daft! I like you going on about Ollie – it makes me laugh. But, yeah, a night out is a fab idea."

"What would you do if you bumped into Kyle though?"

"Snog him, of course. Wouldn't it be great if I started going out with him? Then we could all go out as a foursome together. And I could drone on about Kyle as much as you do about Ollie. What do you say?"

Kerry threw a pillow at Sonja for an answer.

• • •

"No chance. Sorry, Kez, but there's absolutely no way I'd want to do that."

Ollie looked into Kerry's earnest eyes and, seeing the look of disappointment in them, immediately regretted what he'd said. They were walking hand in hand through the park and Kerry had just told him about her conversation with Sonja the previous evening.

He had listened sympathetically. He'd agreed that Kerry shouldn't drift away from her best friend because of him, and had laughed out loud when Kerry mentioned that Sonja had accused her of 'droning on about her boyfriend'.

But when she'd mentioned Kyle and the

possibility of them going out in a foursome together – even though Sonja and Kyle weren't even an item yet – Ollie's face had clouded over. He dismissed the suggestion so emphatically that Kerry almost felt as if she'd just asked him to gouge out his eyes with a blunt instrument.

"Honestly, Kerry, it's not that I'm against going out in a foursome in principal. It's just that I'm 99 per cent sure I know of this Kyle and, believe me, he's a complete waste of space. Sonja would be mad to get involved with him."

Kerry stopped in her tracks and stood in front of Ollie, her eyes searching his face for clues.

"What do you mean?" she demanded. "How do you know him? I've only told you his name. How do you know we're talking about the same guy?"

"Well, for a start, how many guys do you know called Kyle around here? There can't be too many of them walking around Winstead, can there?"

"Er, no, I guess not. So what do you know about him? He must have done something pretty awful for you to bad-mouth him like that. It's not your style at all."

Ollie turned towards Kerry, a serious expression on his usually cheerful face. "Maybe I'm being a bit harsh, but I just think the guy is bad news. If

Sonja's looking for a quick fling then fine, but believe me, he won't hang around once he's got what he wants. He's like it with all girls. She'd be better off steering well clear of him."

His words of warning ringing in her ears, Kerry wondered how she should break the news to Sonja.

But it was already too late.

CHAPTER 4

•••••••••••••••••••••••••••

BOYWATCH

By the time Kerry had got up and left the Harveys'
house on Sunday morning, Sonja had already
mentally put the finishing touches to her Kyle-
catching plan. There was no time to lose if she
was going to win her bet with Catrina, which she
was determined to do.

Although she knew little about him other than
his name and the fact that he worked in the new
sports shop in the Plaza, Sonja figured it would be
a good test of her initiative to discover more. The
obvious place to start was the Plaza. She was
pretty sure the sports shop would be open on a
Sunday.

Sonja had decided a while ago that it was
about time she had a boyfriend. She hadn't had
any serious love interest for months. Most people

28

who knew her considered Sonja to be a ten out of ten on the babe-o-meter. *Easily*. She had long blonde hair, penetrating blue eyes, perfect bone structure, a figure to die for and great dress sense. She literally turned heads in the street.

When she thought about it, Sonja realised that she probably was too fussy. But rightly so. She had no intention of going out with just anyone. Most of the guys who came into contact with her and who fancied their chances were given the knock back. Politely, of course.

But Sonja was no wilting wallflower either. If she saw someone she fancied, she had no qualms about going straight over and chatting them up. Not in a full-on way like Catrina, but *subtly*, sussing out whether they had a brain behind the good looks.

She was quite measured in her approach to guys – they had to be good-looking, but if there wasn't a spark in the conversation as well, forget it. She didn't have the time to waste on pretty – but vacant – faces.

The dilemma with Kyle was that they'd never actually met. Somehow she was going to have to find a way to chat him up in the shop or in the street. Even super-assured Sonja found that prospect daunting. Hence the need for a plan, which she was now ready to put into action.

Pulling her bright red paddle brush through her hair, Sonja glanced at herself in the full-length mirror in the hallway and gave herself a quick once-over.

Straight-cut jeans, strappy low-heeled sandals, a bright blue T-shirt, lightly bronzed skin and no make-up other than a touch of lip gloss was as much effort as Sonja felt she needed to make. It was as much effort as she *ever* made, not being into the tarty clothes nor caked-on make-up look (hence the scene with Cat on Saturday night).

"You'll do," she muttered to herself as she grabbed her bag from the sideboard and headed for the front door.

The stroll through town to the centre of Winstead on such a fabulously hot day was uplifting. She almost forgot her reason for going as she breathed in the heat and listened to the gentle breeze rustling the trees. Being a Sunday, the roads were quieter than normal, and what traffic did pass by seemed to be moving at a much slower pace, in keeping with the laid-back feel of the day.

When Sonja got to the Plaza, Winstead's shopping centre, she went inside and wandered towards the new sports shop, looking in casually as she passed.

Unable to see Kyle, she sauntered on to the

little café at the centre of the mall and ordered a cappuccino. Then she sat down and spent the next twenty minutes watching the world go by.

Just as she decided it was time to head back and go right into the shop this time, Sonja saw Kyle wander right past her. Wow! He looked tastier than ever. And, even better, he seemed to be on his own. Perfect! Time to put her plan into action.

Before he was able to get too far away from her, Sonja leapt up from her seat and chased after him.

"Ben! Ben! Wait up!" she called as she sped towards Kyle's rapidly disappearing (and very cute) rear.

Not surprisingly, he didn't turn round. Directly behind him now, Sonja reached up and tapped him on the shoulder.

"Ben?" she said again. He stopped and turned to her, a confused look on his face.

"Oh! I'm sorry!" said Sonja, smiling sweetly, then looking at the ground in a show of embarrassment.

Returning her gaze to his, she added, "I thought you were someone else."

Kyle looked moderately taken aback but pleased at the same time as he took in the vision standing in front of him.

"Sorry to disappoint you," he grinned, blushing. "I could change my name if that's any help…"

Sonja smiled back and thought, *So far so good*. "That's OK – and it's not a disappointment."

Anyone else would have cringed at such a line, but not Sonja. She was confident enough to carry it off and make it sound like the most sincere thing she had ever said.

And Kyle certainly seemed to appreciate it. His grin just got broader, his face got redder with embarrassment and his eyes popped even further out of his head as he so obviously thought, *Wow, what a babe!*

"So, uh… were you supposed to be meeting this Ben here, then?" he asked, trying to keep the conversation going.

"Ooh, no, I came into town *on my own*," answered Sonja pointedly. "Ben's the boyfriend of a friend of mine and you just looked like him from the back."

"Oh, right."

They stopped talking and looked at each other for a moment, then Kyle picked up the conversation again.

"Uh, it's my lunchbreak… I was actually just heading off for a coffee. D'you fancy one?"

"Mmm, that'd be great," replied Sonja, thinking, *Yeesss, I'm in here!*

Kyle looked over Sonja's shoulder and spotted the café-bar she'd just come from in the distance. "Is that place OK for you?" he said coolly.

"Fine."

They retraced their steps back to the café and Kyle motioned to the very table Sonja had been sitting at a few minutes before.

"I'll get them," he said, digging his hand into his jeans pocket. "What d'you fancy?"

Apart from you, you mean? thought Sonja naughtily. "I'll have a cappuccino, please," she smiled brightly then sat down and watched him as he sauntered up to the counter.

Such a cute bum! she thought. *I can't believe how well this is going.*

"So, I haven't seen you around Winstead before," she lied when he came back with the coffees. "Are you here on holiday?"

Kyle blinked at her a couple of times then opened his mouth and laughed. "Er, no," he replied, "I live here, always have done. I work in the new sports shop – it's just back there. Do you know it?"

"Oh!" Sonja replied, all fake surprise. "Well, I've walked past it a few times. But I don't think I've seen you in there."

"Maybe because until a week ago my hair was a lot longer and mostly covered my face, so you

might just have missed me hidden under there. And, of course, I looked like a bit of a dork."

"Oh, I can't believe that," smiled Sonja. She watched him study her every move as she sipped her coffee.

He looked totally smitten.

CHAPTER 5

●●●●●●●●●●●●●●●●●●●●●●●●●●●●●●

MISSION ACCOMPLISHED

"Honestly, guys, it couldn't have been easier. He might as well have had a sign on top of his head that said 'Ask Me Out'. I swear, his chin nearly hit the floor when I invited him to go to the pictures with me on Friday night. I've never picked up such an easy date in my life."

Sonja was sitting at the window table in the End-of-the-Line café relaying yesterday's encounter with Kyle to Catrina, Matt, Kerry and Joe in great detail.

She was still on a high from the meeting, not only because her plan had worked out perfectly, but because Kyle had been such a pushover. Once she'd realised he was interested (in about a millisecond), the rest had been easy.

They had chatted at the café for about twenty

minutes, by which time they'd swapped phone numbers and arranged a night out together.

Kerry kept quiet, her stomach in her boots as she listened to Sonja babble on. After her conversation with Ollie, she'd intended to have a quiet word with her friend while they were all at the End. But it was too late. Sonja wouldn't thank her for announcing that the first guy she'd had the hots for in ages was bad news. Who would? Kerry decided to keep the knowledge to herself for a while longer and pick another time to say something. If at all.

"So, the upshot of all this," Sonja continued, turning to her cousin, "is that I win the bet from Saturday night. Remember, Cat?"

Catrina gave Sonja a cool stare. "Uh-oh, I don't think so," she replied. "I mean, you haven't actually gone out with him yet. Just because he's said yes doesn't mean he'll turn up."

"Oh come *on*," snorted Sonja. "Like he's going to stand *me* up."

"He might not have had his contact lenses in yesterday," Catrina shot back. "When he sees what you really look like, he'll run a mile."

"Don't judge other people by your own experiences, Catrina," Sonja said, enjoying the sparring match. "Just because you have to go out with a bag over your head in order to get a date."

"Now, now, girls, can we have an end to this bickering, please?" Matt Ryan interrupted, his arms outstretched as if to keep the cousins (who were sitting on either side of him) apart. "I think most of us came here for a drink and a chat *among friends*, not to witness World War Three breaking out. Now, who's for another coffee – I'm buying."

Matt took everyone's order and strode up to the stainless-steel serving counter. Behind the scenes, the End looked deserted.

"Hello?" Matt called. "Anyone there?" He heard a clattering noise coming from the depths of the kitchen then saw Anna Michaels hurrying towards him, wiping her hands on a towel.

"Sorry, Matt," she called. "Ollie's working next door, so I'm here on my own. I was just making up some sandwiches. What can I get you?"

Giving Matt a big smile, she brushed a few stray hairs away from her face and pulled a notepad from the pocket of her apron.

"Two coffees, one cappuccino, a Diet Coke, a strawberry milkshake and whatever you're having. Then why don't you take five minutes and come over and join us?" Matt winked and gave Anna his sexiest grin.

"Thanks, Matt," she said. "I'll have a coffee. And if we don't get a rush on in the next few

minutes, I'll take you up on the offer of a sit-down. I'll bring them over when they're ready."

Anna watched him swagger back to the others and smiled to herself. Matt was so super-smooth in such an obvious way that he almost made her die laughing at times. But she couldn't help liking him all the same.

As Anna got a tray and started to get the order together, she realised how surprising it was that she did like Matt. Outwardly, he seemed brash and arrogant, much like David, her ex.

David had been half the reason why she had run away from her old life over a year ago. And it was partly down to him that Anna found it difficult to depend on anyone any more; she had taken such an emotional battering that she'd lost her faith in human nature.

Anna wondered if she would ever feel like a normal person again. She doubted it. It was amazing to think how much she had changed; not long ago she had been a regular, happy, sixteen-year-old, living at home, going to college, with little to concern her other than which of her friends to go out with on a Saturday night.

Just over a year later and she no longer recognised the carefree, living for laughs girl she had once been. Today, Anna Michaels felt a good decade older than she ought to: worldly-wise and

wary, cautious and insular. Independent, yes, but also very lonely. Since leaving home, she had moved around a bit before arriving in Winstead where she'd found the job in the café and settled in the flat above. Slowly, her life was getting back on to an even keel.

But as she looked up and watched Matt and his friends larking about, Anna felt a desperate need to belong. In the few months since she had moved to Winstead, the opportunities to get involved with real life again had been there. She had grown fond of Matt's particular crowd and felt that they had all gone out of their way to make her welcome. One day soon she hoped she'd be ready to open up and let them in.

But not yet.

• • •

"So what do you think? The pink top from here or the purple cross-over from Miss Selfridge?"

Sonja stood in the middle of What She Wants and demanded Kerry's opinion. Even though Kerry was working at the chemist's, Sonja had managed to cajole her into spending her Wednesday lunch hour traipsing round Winstead's shopping centre to help her find something to wear for her date on Friday night.

"I mean," Sonja went on, "the purple's definitely more my colour, don't you think? But the pink one's a bit less smart. And I don't want to turn up looking like I'm dressed for The Ritz when we're only going to the pictures, do I? That would be so naff, wouldn't it?"

Kerry looked vaguely at the top Sonja was waving about. She was hardly listening. Instead, she was worrying about whether to mention all the stuff Ollie had told her about Kyle. She knew she ought to say something – any true friend would – but she wasn't entirely sure how Sonja would take it. Probably not very well was the niggling thought at the back of her head, and that was why she still hadn't spoken up.

"You haven't been listening to a word I've said," barked Sonja, jerking Kerry back to reality. "Come on," she added, "stop dreaming about Ollie and help me with this. *Please*."

Sonja looked at her friend in desperation. For the first time in her life she was actually nervous about going out with someone. She wasn't sure whether this was because she felt she really liked Kyle or because it was so long since she'd been on a proper date.

Whatever the reason, she was determined to get it right on the night.

"Oh, sorry," Kerry whimpered sheepishly. "I

was miles away. Actually, I prefer the purple one. It's definitely more you."

"Hmmm."

Kerry knew immediately that this was the wrong answer. Sonja merely wanted confirmation of what she had already decided to buy which, judging by the tone of the muffled "Hmmm", was the pink top.

"I'll just go and pay for this then and we can go," said Sonja and walked briskly to the checkout.

Kerry cursed her friend under her breath. What was the point of asking her opinion when Sonja had already made up her mind? It was so typical.

"I'll have to get back now," Kerry said as they walked out of the shop together.

"Oh, right, OK. And thanks for coming with me, Kez. I feel much better getting a second opinion. Y'know, I've got a really good vibe about this date. I can't wait."

Kerry smiled and hugged her friend, then set off back to work for the afternoon. She liked her job at Mr Hardy's but it could be a bit boring and routine at times.

This particular afternoon was going incredibly slowly. Apart from a man coming in to buy haemorrhoid cream at about three o'clock, there were hardly any other customers at all. Then, just

as Mr Hardy was locking the medical supplies in their cabinets at the back of the shop before shutting up for the evening, a young lad came in.

Kerry went to serve him. She thought she vaguely recognised him as he browsed his way up to the counter, but she couldn't be sure. As he handed her a prescription which she passed through the hatch to Mr Hardy, she took a quick look at it: it was made out to Kyle Marsdon.

Oh my God! she thought. *It's him!*

She watched agog as he inspected the shelves around him. She could see what Sonja saw in him – he was definitely cute. Then her mouth gaped as he began studying the condoms to the left of the cash till.

Oh, no, he's not going to buy condoms – surely! she thought, her face reddening. *He's going on a first date with my best friend on Friday and he's standing here about to buy condoms.*

Kerry was aghast. She could hardly bear to watch, but she couldn't look away either. Eyes still glued to Kyle, but desperate not to have to believe what she was seeing, she scurried to the opposite end of the counter. In her rush, she tripped over a cardboard box she'd been taking stock from earlier.

"Ouerrff!" Kerry found herself sprawled on her side on the shop floor, the box flattened beneath

her. She lay there for a few seconds, dazed and uncoordinated. Then, her face burning even redder, she scrambled up to a sitting position and quickly adjusted her glasses which were hanging off the end of her nose. As she looked up, a face appeared from the other side of the counter.

"Are you all right?" Kyle asked anxiously.

Kerry opened her mouth to speak but found that no words would come out. Instead she sat guppy-like and humiliated, wishing she was somewhere – anywhere – else.

Kyle rushed round to her side of the counter, concern written on his face. Squatting in front of Kerry, he held out his arms and took her by the hands.

"Come on, let's get you up," he commanded, "so we can check there aren't any broken bones."

Not daring to look him in the eye, Kerry meekly allowed Kyle to haul her on to her feet.

"I... uh... thanks," she croaked.

Just then Mr Hardy walked out from his dispensary at the back of the shop.

"Kerry! What on earth is going on here? And what are you doing letting your boyfriend behind the counter? You know it's forbidden to let anyone around here."

The shock of his words stung Kerry into stupefied silence once more. Mr Hardy must have

heard the commotion and got the wrong idea. Completely.

Understandable, though. They probably looked like a couple of star-crossed lovers standing there hand in hand. *He* wasn't to know the whole story, walking in on the tail end of it like that. Kerry whipped her hands out of Kyle's, folded them defensively across her chest, and immediately made herself look even more guilty.

Fortunately, Kyle came to the rescue.

"Oh, no, Sir, it's not what you think," he explained, a look of open honesty on his face. "I don't know this girl at all. She tripped and fell over – I just came round here to make sure she wasn't hurt."

Mr Hardy looked suspiciously from Kyle to Kerry and back again. Then his face softened slightly and he muttered something about Mr Marsdon's prescription being ready before disappearing into the dispensary.

"Thanks again," Kerry finally managed, looking up at Kyle and noticing his eyes twinkling with mirth.

"That's okay," he said lightly. "Are you sure you're all right?"

"I'm fine thanks. Really... I'll, uh, get your prescription."

As she backed away towards the little hatch to

pick up his goods, he moved back to where he had originally been standing in front of the condoms. Kerry stared transfixed as he reached out and picked up two packets of throat sweets from the shelf in front of the condom display. He handed them to her.

"Sore throat," he said. "Had it for over a week, but nothing seems to get rid of it. Think I'll give these a go."

Kerry nodded and smiled, and cursed herself for having an overactive imagination.

CHAPTER 6

● ●

SONJA'S FIRST DATE

For about the fifteenth time so far, Sonja stood in front of her full-length bedroom mirror and wrinkled her nose in distaste. It didn't matter what she tried on, none of her clothes looked right.

Even the pink top that had looked so fabulous in the shop now looked garish and out of place next to anything she put with it.

The fact was Sonja was suffering from a massive bout of PMS and therefore her usual confidence had dissolved into gloomy self-criticism. It was amazing how one day and a few nagging hormones could turn even someone like her into a gibbering, cranky no-hoper. Sighing dramatically, she climbed out of the blue baggy shirt and cream shorts she was wearing and

grabbed something else from the mountain of clothes strewn about her bed.

Half an hour later and she had finally decided to go back to the shirt and shorts, not least because it wouldn't be long before she had to leave to meet Kyle for their date. Once dressed, but refusing to study her clothes any more in case she didn't get out of the house at all, Sonja got up close to her reflection and frowned at her face: at least there weren't any zits erupting from her skin. At the moment.

Cursing herself for having the pre-period blues, she vowed not to waste any more time on negative thoughts, grabbed her bag, and left.

Sonja reached the cinema with only minutes to spare. She'd expected Kyle to be waiting for her – but he wasn't there. She gritted her teeth and seethed inside, imagining her foul-tempered hormones rushing to the surface. Then, getting a grip on her temper, she tried to think rationally.

Was she missing something? Had they perhaps said seven-thirty rather than seven-fifteen? She looked at the poster advertising the film they were supposed to be seeing. No, that couldn't be it: the film *started* at seven thirty... in about five minutes in fact. *Grrr!* This didn't bode well for the future.

Just then she felt a gentle tap on her shoulder.

Spinning round, she came nose to nose with Kyle. Sonja stared at him, refusing to let her face register anything other than a stony glare which she hoped he would have the sense to read as a look of irritated displeasure.

"Oh, God, Sonja, I'm *so* sorry," muttered Kyle. His brow furrowed into deep lines and he raked his left hand through his blond hair in the cutest of cute ways (or at least, that's what Sonja thought, as her heart melted from a block of ice to a rushing waterfall).

"My car's in the garage being repaired so I had to rely on the bus and it was late. I really am sorry..."

He gave Sonja a deeply apologetic look and she forgave him instantly.

"Anyway," he continued, "shall we go in or we'll miss the beginning."

"Sure."

Sonja put her arm confidently through Kyle's and they walked up the steps together.

• • •

"So, d'you fancy getting something to eat?" Kyle asked as he and Sonja strolled hand in hand through the streets of Winstead later that evening.

"Yeah, I'm starving. There's a little Italian called Luigi's just round the corner from here which is supposed to be really cosy. We could go there."

"Er... well, actually, I'm a bit strapped for cash at the moment. I was thinking maybe we could get a burger from Fat Larry's – he's usually parked in the lay-by by the Plaza on a Friday night. His fried onion rings are unbeatable."

Sonja tried hard to hide her disappointment as she was steered down the road towards the mobile burger bar. It had been a really great evening so far; they had roared with laughter in exactly the same places in the film, and held hands and shared popcorn and Coke. They had discussed the movie on the way out of the cinema and, amazingly, were in total agreement about it.

Sonja had thought that the perfect way to round off the evening would be to go to the cheap but romantic-looking restaurant she'd heard about – she had even made a quick detour to check that it was open on her way to the cinema.

But now..?

Well, who says a greasy hot dog and fries can't be just as romantic? she thought as she walked towards Fat Larry's van with its neon sign flashing on and off in an oddly disconcerting manner.

After all, the person you're with is more important than the place you're in.

Sonja tried hard to find something that looked appetising from the fare Fat Larry (for that's who she assumed the large man behind the counter was) served up, but ended up ordering just fries and a portion of onion rings (on Kyle's insistence). In the meantime he had the works: double cheeseburger, large fries, double onion rings and a couple of deep fried pineapple rings to finish off.

They then sat on a wooden bench overlooking the High Street and ate their takeaway.

Kyle kept Sonja entertained while they ate, asking her about herself, yet keeping the conversation light by telling her jokes and funny anecdotes about himself in between mouthfuls of food.

He made her laugh by wearing his pineapple rings as earrings – childish, she knew, but somehow cute all the same. Sonja found herself liking him more all the time, with his cheekily dimpled face, ready smile and succulent lips (which she was dying to kiss).

When he had polished off his food, and most of hers, they walked arm in arm along the street, looking in shop windows, chatting easily about nothing in particular. When they came to a travel

agent's Kyle stopped and began poring over the numerous cards in the window.

"You know, I've never been further than the Isle of Wight," he said wistfully. "I've never been abroad. The nearest I've got to being on a plane has been watching it on the telly. I can't imagine what it's like to fly."

Sonja, who usually went abroad at least twice a year, even if only to visit relatives in Sweden, adored flying. "Oh, you'd love it," she enthused. "It's the oddest, most wonderfully weird feeling in the world."

"I'm sure it is," answered Kyle. "When I was little my dad used to take me to see the planes at Heathrow. We used to stand in the viewing gallery for hours watching them take off and land. He promised me that one day we'd be on one together, jetting off to the other side of the world."

"He hasn't got around to it yet then?" Sonja asked.

"No, and he won't now. He died a couple of years back. Cancer."

"Oh," Sonja said in a small voice. "I'm sorry."

"S'OK," he said, turning to her with a serious look on his face for the first time since she'd met him. "We had plenty of warning. It was on the cards for months before he went. Better that way

than for it to happen suddenly. That's what I think anyway."

Sonja bit her lip and said nothing. She hadn't expected the evening to move on like this; it showed another dimension to Kyle, one which she wouldn't normally expect a guy to reveal so early on in a relationship. It made her fall for him all the more.

• • •

"Why don't you come back to my place for a coffee?" Kyle asked as they walked along the road together later.

"Um, thanks for the offer, but I really ought to get back home. Another time maybe..."

Even though they were getting on really well, Sonja hardly knew Kyle; there was no way she was going back to his flat with him right now, no matter how much she fancied him.

"Are you sure?" he persisted. "I mean, it's not far from here. We could walk there, then I'll call you a cab home. I don't bite. Honest."

He turned to face her, gave her a winning smile then lowered his head to kiss her.

Sonja could feel her heart pounding as she raised her head to respond. When his lips met hers a zing of excitement shot through her entire

body like an electric shock and she melted into him. It was heavenly.

They stood and kissed for ever; she felt his lips kissing hers, then she melted some more as his mouth butterfly-kissed her cheek, her nose and her eyes, first one then the other. She felt his hands travel up and down her back, gently kneading her skin with the tips of his fingers. Then they made their way round to her waist and up to the buttons of her shirt.

Oh, my God, he's going for my boobs! she thought suddenly in alarm. *What does he think he's doing?* Pulling her mouth away from his, Sonja lifted her hands – which had been resting comfortably on the waistband of Kyle's jeans – and slammed them protectively over her chest.

"I don't think so!" Sonja said firmly.

From the look on his face, Kyle was obviously taken aback. Then he tapped his hands together like he was praying and gave her a cheeky grin.

"I'm really sorry, Son," he smiled, eyes twinkling mischievously. "I got a bit carried away. You're just so hot, I couldn't help myself. I don't know what came over me."

Sonja wasn't entirely convinced. "Well, try a bit of self-control next time, will you? I'm not that kind of girl, you know," she said and strode purposefully up the road.

"Yeah, sure. Sorry. I never thought you were. Like I said, I just... well, you know. I apologise. Do you forgive me?" Kyle gave her an imploring puppy-dog look that begged instant forgiveness.

"So long as you don't try anything like that again."

"Whatever you say, Son. From now on, you call the shots."

As they continued walking towards Sonja's house, she felt a strange surge of excitement and trepidation at the same time. She couldn't help wondering what she was letting herself in for.

CHAPTER 7

●●●●●●●●●●●●●●●●●●●●●●●●●●●●●

WHO'S THE HUNK?

"Wow! What a guy! He's obviously been taking lessons from me!"

Matt curled up on the long banquette at the End and roared with laughter as Sonja relayed the full details of her first date with Kyle.

"I mean, it wasn't as though I was surprised he tried it on," she went on, while her friend sniggered into his hands. "After all, *some* guys feel like the evening's not complete unless they have a go. What got to me more than anything was the fact that he had his hands all over me *in the street*, where anyone could see. It's bad enough having someone grope you on a first date, but even tackier when they try it on in public."

"I can't believe he would dare to do that," mumbled Joe sympathetically, secretly wondering

what it would be like to have the nerve to try it on with a girl like that.

"Maybe you gave him the wrong vibes," Matt said, trying to be helpful. "Maybe he thought he could buy you – a portion of onion rings in exchange for a quick grope." His voice cracked as he spoke and his face creased up into howls of laughter again. Joe giggled nervously.

"Well, thanks for the sympathy, Matt," said Sonja. "I'm so pleased I've told you. I was hoping I might get a sensible male viewpoint on this one, but obviously I momentarily forgot I was dealing with a moron."

"Sorry, Son," laughed Matt. "But the thought of Sonja Harvey being romanced at Fat Larry's is hilarious. It's like promising the Queen Mum a slap-up meal and then taking her to Burger King. You just wouldn't do it."

"Actually, that bit didn't bother me, although it made me realise Kyle's probably about as romantic as a dead trout. It was just the mauling bit that got to me. The rest of the evening was brill."

"Did he try it on again when he got you home?" Joe asked.

"No," Sonja shook her head. "We had another snog on my doorstep, but I didn't invite him in. I didn't want him to think he could jump on me

again. He said he'd call me then left to get the bus home."

"Hmmm." Matt scratched his chin with one hand and drummed his fingers on the table with the other. "For what it's worth, and being totally serious now, I think he was testing you, seeing how far he could push you on a first date. If you'd gone much further he would have thought you were easy. So he would have arranged another date fairly promptly, had his wicked way with you and then lost interest."

Sonja tutted loudly.

"But the fact that you stopped him was good," continued Matt. "It will have kept him keen on you, but made him realise you're no pushover. He'll respect you more for that. If you're really lucky, you might even get a relationship out of him."

"God, it's really sad if that's how guys' minds work," Sonja sighed. "Or is it just the way *your* sordid little brain thinks things through?"

Matt guffawed again. "It's certainly how I'd view the situation, but I can't speak for the rest of the male population. You'd have to ask someone else, like Joe. No, don't ask Joe – you wouldn't have a clue, would you, Joey?"

Joe searched frantically for words to defend himself but could think of nothing. He hated it

when one of the others zeroed in on him like this, and the truth was he had no defence. So he merely sat and grunted at Matt.

"You could ask Ollie for his opinion," Matt continued, "but what he has with Kerry is pretty special, so he might not be a good bet either."

"What's that about me and Ollie?"

Matt and Sonja turned round to see Kerry standing in the open doorway of the café, looking suspicious.

"Oh, hi, Kez, take a seat. Son will explain everything." Matt looked gleefully at Sonja as Kerry slid into the seat opposite her.

"Has she told you about her hot date with Kyle?" Matt continued, relishing the prospect of taking the mick out of Sonja some more.

"Er, no," Kerry replied, still looking anxious. "Was it OK, Son? Did you try to phone? I wasn't in last night. Ol and I went for something to eat..."

"He didn't take you to Fat Larry's, did he?" smirked Matt then yelped as he felt the toe of Sonja's sandal kick him in the calf.

"I've been dying to know what happened," Kerry continued, ignoring Matt. "Did you have a good time?"

Sonja retold her story, aided and abetted by numerous interruptions and smart-arse comments

from Matt, while Kerry listened intently. Joe, who was sitting next to Kerry, fiddled nervously with a sachet of sugar and daydreamed about kissing her.

By the time Sonja (and Matt) had finished, Kerry was sitting with her hands over her eyes and her mouth gaping, an expression of amused shock on her face.

"He must have some nerve," she spluttered, "to steam in there like that on a first date. I'd be really angry if anyone tried to do that with me. I can't believe it!"

"But the thing is, Kez," Sonja began to explain, "he's got so much charm and he does everything with a huge grin on his face, you can't help but like him. He's the sort who'll sail through his life getting exactly what he wants from people just by giving them that winning smile."

"I know exactly what you mean," said Kerry, and finally told them about her encounter with Kyle in the chemist's shop, even admitting how she had been convinced he was going to buy condoms rather than throat sweets.

"Most incredibly of all," she ended as the others chuckled at her story, "he won Mr Hardy over instantly. If it had been anyone else behind the counter with me, I would have been given the sack on the spot. But Kyle just smiled at him,

called him 'Sir' and explained what had happened. And it worked. The only one who looked like a berk was me. Kyle must have thought I was a right idiot from the way I acted."

"I can't believe your mind was so sordid as to think he was buying condoms in the first place," Matt tutted. "You're not as innocent as you make out, Kerry Bellamy."

Kerry blushed slightly and wished she'd waited till she and Sonja were alone before revealing her own meeting with Kyle.

"Don't take any notice of him," Sonja reassured her. "He's a fine one to talk. So you liked Kyle then? Cute, isn't he?"

"Mmm," Kerry nodded vigorously. "Very. I can see why you fancy him."

"Well, hands off, he's mine," Sonja joked. Standing up, she began edging her way out of the banquette and stood at the end of their table.

"Now, I must go to the loo," she carried on. "Shall I get more Cokes while I'm up?"

The others nodded and Sonja gave her order to Dorothy, who worked part-time at the café. Then she noticed a guy she'd never seen before sitting on his own at a table near the toilets.

Wow, he's gorgeous! she thought and slowed her pace a little in the hope that he might notice her. However, he seemed intent on staring into

his drink and didn't even look up as she swept open the door to the loos.

When Sonja came back, he was still there, only now he was staring out of the window, completely oblivious to her.

"Hey, have you seen the bloke sitting on his own over there?" she hissed to Kerry when she got back to her seat. "At the table nearest the loo. Budge up a bit so you can get a better look."

Kerry shuffled along the seat until the lad in question came into view.

"Oh, yes," she said. "I haven't seen him in here before. I wonder who he is."

"Never mind that," scolded Sonja. "Would you just look at him? He's *seriously* tasty."

"What are you two whispering about?" demanded Matt in an overly loud voice.

"Ssssh! Keep it down," Sonja hissed. "We're eyeballing a gorgeous hunk."

"You mean *you're* eyeballing him," Kerry corrected. "I'm just a casual observer."

Matt and Joe looked over to where the girls were staring.

"What is it with you at the moment, Sonja?" Matt teased. "You're rampant."

"I know, it must be the hormones. But look at him. Have you ever seen anyone so hunky in your life?"

"Nah, he's not my type," replied Matt. "He's a bit butch-looking for me."

"Do you think he's waiting for someone?" Sonja carried on. "Or is he just killing time before he catches a train or something?"

"Does it really matter?" asked Matt.

"Oh yes, of course. I mean, if he's on his own then there's nothing to stop me from going over and chatting him up, is there?"

"Face it, Son," Matt continued, "the mood you're in, there's nothing to stop you from doing that anyway."

"You know what? That's the most intelligent thing you've said all morning," beamed Sonja. "I'm going to go right over and talk to him."

She got up and strode purposefully over to the other side of the café.

CHAPTER 8

● ●

CHAT-UP NUMBER TWO

The good thing about the table nearest the toilet was that it was next to Nick, the café owner's, old jukebox. This gave Sonja the perfect excuse to be within talking distance of Tasty Guy, without having to stand in front of him and strike up a conversation from nowhere.

Checking the contents of her purse, Sonja walked casually over to the jukebox, aware that at least two pairs of eyes were on her, if not more (she hoped). She glanced at Tasty Guy as she walked and was disappointed to note that he was staring into the distance rather than at her.

On closer inspection he was even better-looking. He had tanned skin and dark brown hair, the colour of Bourneville chocolate. His nose was small and neat, his mouth big and plump, and his

eyes (what she could see of them hidden beneath a long fringe), well, they had to be dark. He looked how Sonja imagined all the swashbuckling heroes were in the romantic novels her mum read. Except that this one was real.

Standing side on to him at the jukebox, Sonja rummaged in her purse, then tutted loudly to herself. She turned to Tasty Guy.

"Excuse me, but you don't have any change for this, do you?"

Tasty Guy looked as though he'd been shaken out of a particularly engrossing dream as his head shot up and his eyes focused in Sonja's direction.

"Sorry?"

Sonja gave him her most winning smile. "The jukebox," she carried on. "You don't have any tens or fifties for it, do you?" She held up a pound coin in case he still didn't get what she was talking about.

"Oh, right. Sorry…" He half stood up and stuck his hand in the front pocket of his jeans, pulled out the contents and let them scatter on to the table in front of him: a screwed-up piece of paper, an elastic band, some loose change, an X Files key ring, an ancient-looking Polo mint, a grey, raggedy hanky…

"Blimey, a psychologist would have a field day studying that lot," commented Sonja lightly.

He chuckled, as much to himself as to her, she thought.

"What was it you were after again?" he asked.

"Uh, change for a pound?" she said hopefully.

"Sorry, can't do it," he said as he gathered up the coins and began counting them out. "How much is it per go?"

"Twenty pence."

"Here you are." He nudged two twenties across the table towards her. "One play for you and one for me."

"Great, thanks," Sonja grinned. "So long as you realise there isn't much on here after 1975. Nick's a bit of an old fossil, I'm afraid."

Tasty Guy suddenly looked much more alert. "Nick?" he asked. "Is he the owner of this place?"

"Yeah," Sonja said. "He owns the record shop next door too."

"Do you know him then?"

"Oh, yeah, everyone knows Nick. What do you fancy? On the jukebox I mean?"

"Uh... anything. You choose. Is he here today?"

Sonja didn't answer; instead she tapped digits into the jukebox to a couple of rock classics she hoped would impress him. She turned back to Tasty Guy.

"No," she finally answered. "Nick's probably

next door. Are you looking for a job or something?"

He shook his head and motioned her to sit down. "No, I'm hoping to catch up with someone I thought worked here. Her name's Anna. You don't know her as well, do you?"

"Of course. But she's not in until later. Are you a friend of hers?"

Tasty Guy hesitated. "Uh... kind of."

"Oh," Sonja said. She had been hoping for a fuller answer. "By the way, I'm Sonja."

He smiled up at her. "Pleased to meet you, Sonja."

She had been expecting him to tell her his name too, but he didn't, so she continued digging for information.

"So how do you know Anna?"

Tasty Guy shifted uneasily in his seat. "Oh, we go back a long way," he said vaguely. "You don't know where she lives, do you? I mean, I'd really like to see her and, rather than hanging around, I could go and look her up at home."

Although Anna lived in the flat above the café, Sonja instinctively felt it would be wrong to pass on this information to someone she'd never laid eyes on before. Particularly as he seemed to be showing such an interest in Anna's whereabouts. She had to think fast.

"To be honest, I remember her saying she'd be out all morning. But I can try and find out for you if you like."

"Only if you're sure it's no bother..."

Sonja was keen to help such a sweet guy as much as possible. "Not at all. I'll see what I can do. And if she's out there's plenty to do in Winstead if you need to kill a few hours. I could show you around, if you like."

He gave her a mouth-watering smile. "That'd be great. I'd really like that."

Her heart in her mouth, Sonja turned around and headed out of the café. As she passed Matt, Joe and Kerry (who had been straining their ears in a vain attempt to hear the conversation above the music) she gave them the thumbs up. As far as the confident Sonja was concerned, this guy was hers for the taking.

She made her way round to the back of the café where a green wooden door led to a tiny yard and the steps to Anna's flat. Although Sonja had become reasonably friendly with Anna since she'd moved in, she had never actually been round to the flat before. She certainly hadn't been invited inside, and as far as she was aware, no one else had either.

She wondered what Tasty Guy's relationship was with the friendly but reserved Anna. Funny,

he'd never told her his name, though she'd told him hers.

Perhaps he was an old boyfriend. In all the time that Anna had been in Winstead, she had never really mentioned her past – the life she had before she came here. There was no mention of family, friends, school, nothing really.

Sonja wasn't sure if she was being deliberately vague when anyone had tried to draw information out of her, or whether it was because she was shy and reticent, which was how she often came across. Maybe Tasty Guy would shed some light on what had up to now been a very grey area.

Sonja climbed the metal stairs to Anna's flat and pressed the doorbell long and hard.

In the tiny sitting room, Anna nearly jumped out of her skin.

CHAPTER 9

●●●●●●●●●●●●●●●●●●●●●●●●●●●●

ANNA'S MYSTERY MAN

Since moving to Winstead, Anna Michaels was happier than she had been for ages. She felt really settled.

For the most part she loved the fact that no one knew who she was, where she came from, or what her background was. She liked it that all her secrets remained just that. She could reinvent herself if she wanted to, be anyone she liked, from any walk of life.

As it was, she hadn't told any lies about herself, but then she hadn't told many truths either.

Half the reason she preferred to keep in the background was to avoid getting embroiled in other people's lives. But, more importantly, it was also to prevent them getting involved in hers. She

was happy to remain on the sidelines, listening but not getting in too deep. Observing rather than being observed.

For the moment it suited her. One day she might begin to let people in again, but she knew she wasn't ready yet. Until that time, she was prepared to keep up the barriers and remain impenetrable.

The sound of the doorbell rang like an alarm in Anna's head. She immediately put down the self-help book she had been engrossed in and stood up.

Hardly anyone ever called. She could count the number of times on – what, three fingers? – in the four months that she had been here.

The few people she was on friendly terms with – including Nick, café and flat owner – seemed to know not to intrude on her private world upstairs. If they needed to discuss anything with her, they tended to do it while she was at work.

Anna never received post, only the odd piece of junk mail; why would she? No one from her old life knew where she lived.

She had a phone which worked but she never used, and which never rang.

With a huge amount of trepidation, she opened the front door.

Anna felt a wave of relief rush through her

body as she recognised Sonja Harvey standing outside.

"Sonja, hi. What's up?" she greeted the girl with a smile.

"Sorry to bother you on your morning off, but there's someone in the café – a guy – who says he knows you. He wants to see you..."

Anna stopped listening and a feeling of fear gripped her once more. A visitor.

Who could it be? Surely not David. *Please* don't let him have found her.

In a split second a jumble of thoughts flashed through her mind. She toyed with the idea of making some excuses, stuffing a few belongings into a bag and doing a runner.

But she *liked* it here; she didn't want to have to leave. And she didn't want to spend the rest of her life running away...

Sonja's voice broke through her thoughts.

"Anna? Anna – are you OK?

Anna didn't answer. Her mind raced. She could tell Sonja to say she wasn't feeling well... but if it was David, he would only come back now that he knew where she was. Much as she dreaded it, Anna knew her only real option was to face up to her past.

Unable to bring herself to look Sonja in the face, she stared bleakly at the brightly patterned

lino on the floor and mumbled, "Oh. Did he say what he wants?"

"Er... no. He seemed friendly though..." Sonja's voice trailed off. She was concerned by the fear and hostility on Anna's face.

"What does he look like?" Anna demanded.

"Um... just a guy," replied Sonja, feeling less sure of herself now. "Er, I dunno," she continued, "early twenties, tallish, dark hair. What else do you want me to say?"

Anna sighed. It was time to face the music. Perhaps it would be better this way.

"Thanks, Sonja," she said flatly. "I'll come down. But I need to sort myself out first. Could you tell him to give me five minutes?"

• • •

Deep in thought, Sonja made her way back to the front entrance of the End. Anna Michaels really was an oddball, she decided. It was obvious that she wasn't pleased with the idea of someone coming to see her.

What was her problem? Most people would be delighted to have people call round. *Especially* those with few friends and no social life.

She walked back through the open door of the café. Before she could go up to Tasty Guy, who

was still sitting on his own and staring straight at her, she was grabbed by Kerry and steered towards the table by the window where Matt, Joe, and now Maya and Ollie too, sat waiting expectantly.

"Come on," Kerry hissed, "fill us in."

"What?" Sonja frowned, her thoughts still on Anna's weird ways.

"You and that guy. What's going on? Why did you walk out like that? Why is he still here?"

"Oh, right. I'm with you," Sonja said, her train of thought back along the same lines as her friends once more.

She sat down at the table, her back to Tasty Guy, and spoke in a low voice to the expectant faces around her.

"He's come to visit Anna, who I've just been to tell, and I definitely think he's interested."

"What? In Anna?" Ollie asked, disbelief in his voice.

"No, stupid. In me. I could just tell by the way he was looking at me and by the way he spoke. There was a spark between us. Electric. It was instant."

Matt nudged Ollie in the ribs and gave him a wink. "See, I told you mate. She's *rampant*. I think even I might be in with a chance the way she's feeling at the moment."

"You must be joking!" Sonja laughed. "What do you think I am? Desperate?"

"Shall I take that as a no, then?" Matt replied, his face full of mock hurt.

Sonja ignored him. She turned from Kerry to Maya and back again. "You know, I can't believe my luck. No interesting guys around for months, then – boom! – two in the same week. I must be giving off those pheromones."

"Eh?" Matt asked, perplexed. "Ferroro-what?"

"Pheromones," Maya explained. "They're chemicals that animals give off to attract the opposite sex. Sonja obviously has an abundance of them at the moment."

"Got any spare for me?" Matt implored. "I haven't had a snog for hours."

"Get your own." Sonja grinned. "I'm hanging on to mine. There might be loads of other boys out there who are just dying to ask me out. I could even start collecting them."

"So, *has* he asked you out then?" Kerry quizzed, her eyes shining with excitement.

"Um, no, not yet. But I'm sure it's only a matter of time before one of us does the asking. If Anna hadn't been in I was going to show him around town for a few hours until she started her shift. I was quite disappointed when she answered the door."

"Crikey, showing him around Winstead?" Matt mocked. "Apart from boring him stupid, it would only have taken ten minutes. What would you have done for the rest of the time?"

"I'm sure we could have thought of something," Sonja whispered, a mischievous smile lighting up her face. "Now, I must let him know what's happening." She turned to Kerry. "How do I look?"

"Ravishing," Kerry laughed.

"Right, time to go in for the kill. See you later, guys... maybe."

As Sonja walked confidently back to where he was sitting, she noticed something move out of the corner of her eye. Tasty Guy must have seen it too because he turned his gaze away from Sonja over to the serving counter.

Anna stood in the kitchen doorway and scanned the café scene in front of her. When she saw the boy in the corner she started to cry. Huge tears rolled down her crumpled face, then she ran at him and threw herself into his outstretched arms.

Bummer! thought Sonja.

CHAPTER 10

• •

CATCHING UP

Her skin tinged pink with embarrassment, Sonja retreated to the table in the window. She figured dolefully that her pheromones must have run out, or had transferred themselves to Anna instead.

Dammit. She must have completely misread the situation. By the looks of the reunion scene in front of her, they obviously knew each other intimately.

She had noticed the lad's response first. His entire face had broken into a huge grin at the sight of Anna and his eyes lit up like beacons, full of the warmth only people in love have for each other.

And Anna was blubbing like a baby, as if he was someone she hadn't seen for a very long time but whom she had missed like mad.

He *had* to be the love of her life.

Sonja turned from that scene to her friends, who were sitting open-mouthed and gawping.

Talk about getting the wrong end of the stick, she thought. She sat down next to Kerry, by which time Anna and her long-lost friend were also sitting at the little corner table, huddled in animated conversation.

"Oh, well, another one bites the dust," Sonja remarked ruefully and silently thanked God that Cat wasn't there to make snide remarks at her expense.

Mind you, her catty cousin was bound to hear about it – exaggerated a hundred times no doubt – and would take every opportunity from now on to rub her nose in it.

"You don't know that," Kerry said measuredly. "They *might* just be good friends."

"Yeah, and I'm the Queen of Sheba," snorted Sonja. "You can't tell me there isn't some sort of connection between them. She was all over him like a wet towel."

"I have to say I agree with Sonja," Maya said. "They're certainly very close. You can tell by the body..."

"No, you've got it wrong," interrupted Matt. "They're not an item. They can't be. Didn't you notice? That wasn't a snog."

"What?" Sonja grimaced. "Is that what you were looking at, you old perv?"

"No, really," continued Matt, quite indignant now. "When they kissed, it wasn't on the lips. Honestly, I saw it all. It was definitely a cheek to cheek kiss. They're old friends. Or related to each other. Trust me."

"Ssshhh!" Joe warned. "I think we might be about to find out. Anna's coming over."

Anna walked over to the big table by the window and motioned to Ollie. A transformation seemed to have come over her. Her face, which normally looked permanently pinched and sad, now radiated happiness.

For the first time since she'd arrived in Winstead, she looked her true age of eighteen – she could even pass for someone younger – rather than a good fifteen years older.

"Ollie?" she said. "Can I have a word?"

Ollie slid out of the seat and disappeared off to a quiet corner with Anna. The others tried hard to hear but only saw Anna gesticulating wildly and then introducing him to the newcomer. Then Anna and her friend disappeared back into the inner sanctum of the kitchen and Ollie slouched back to his friends.

Turning to Sonja he grinned and said, "Well, guys, his name's Owen. They haven't seen each

other for a long time... and it's OK, Son, you're still in with a chance. He's Anna's brother!"

• • •

"So how did you track me down?"

Anna, curled up like a contented cat on the sofa in her flat, took a slurp of coffee from her mug. She hadn't stopped smiling since she'd first set eyes on her big brother, and her cheeks were flushed and rosy with the pleasure of seeing him for the first time in over a year.

"I tell you, Anna, it wasn't easy. When I heard that you'd upped and left home, with no mention of where you were going, or for how long – or why – I thought I might never see you again." Owen lowered his eyes to the floor and for a moment looked as if he might cry.

"I know. I'm sorry," she said and gave his hand a little squeeze. "That's why I wrote to you. I felt so guilty about not telling you."

"Yeah, and if you hadn't mentioned you were staying with Lucy from school I don't think I would ever have found you. I knew you were staying somewhere in or around Exeter then because that was the postmark on the letter, but that was the only clue you left me. I found out from a friend of mine that Lucy was at university

there. So all I could do was send her a letter via the university and hope it would be passed on."

"Which it obviously was."

"Yeah. Except that by that time you'd moved on again and she didn't know exactly where..."

"Although I did write to her to let her know that I was safe and well and to tell her what I was doing."

"But you didn't give her an address or phone number to contact you. Why was that?"

Anna shrugged. "I guess I wanted to be the one calling the shots. I wanted to sort my life out before I let anyone know exactly where I was."

Owen chuckled. "Well, your theory didn't quite work out, did it? The clues you gave her and which she passed on to me were 'Winstead' and 'working in a café'. Did you know there are seven cafés in Winstead? I know, I've been to them all this morning."

"Oh, Owen, I'm sorry. You've had to do some serious detective work, haven't you? I know I should have contacted you sooner."

"That's OK," he smiled. "I'm here now. You're not mad at me for finding you, are you?"

Anna leaned over and gave Owen the umpteenth big hug of the past half an hour. "Do I look like I'm mad?" she said, eyes sparkling. "We've lost so much time. How did your finals go? Did you pass?"

"Sure, I got a First. You're looking at a fully qualified web designer, and one of several million unemployed graduates looking for someone to give me a job."

"You'll soon be snapped up, I know it. You were always the brainy one. And Cathy – are you still going out with her?"

"Nope. She dumped me for someone else about six months ago."

"Oh no! I thought you were really into her..."

"I was, but so was she." He chuckled. "Nah, I'm well out of it. I'm back on the loose again. Lock up your daughters... Anyway, I haven't travelled this far to talk about me. I want to know what's been going on with you."

"Crikey." Anna took a deep breath and sighed loudly. "Where shall I start? As you can see I'm living in this fancy pad in a smart part of town. And I've got a great career with huge prospects..." She broke off and they both laughed.

"No, really," she went on, "I'm actually dead happy here. I like my job, though it's not the sort of career that's going to set the world alight – although the kitchen's a possibility. I like this flat, I've got to know a few people and they've all been incredibly nice to me. So it's great. I'm quite content. Obviously, I miss you and everyone at home, but, well... things change. People change.

Owen put his coffee mug on the table, took Anna's away and grasped her hands in his. He looked her square in the eye.

"So, are you going to tell me *why* you ran away?"

CHAPTER 11

● ●

ANNA OPENS UP

Anna pulled away from Owen's grasp, folded her arms across her chest and began to rock gently, her eyes shut. An expression of pain was written across her entire face.

I can't tell you, she thought. *I'm not ready*.

Owen stood up, gave her hair a brotherly stroke and went over to the kitchen where an opened bottle of red wine stood on one of the units.

"Fancy a glass?" he asked, lifting the bottle and waving it in front of him.

Anna broke off from her thoughts and looked up. "Mmm, please..." she nodded, adding hesitantly, "has Mum not told you anything then?"

Owen frowned, shook his head and began

rummaging in the cupboards for wine glasses.

Maybe I can tell him a few things, Anna thought as she watched him, *but not everything. I can't tell him the whole truth.* Owen removed the cork half poking from the bottle, poured the wine and handed a glass to Anna. As he sat down, she took a swift gulp and began her story.

"I wouldn't say I ran away exactly," she said. "It was more the case that I had to leave."

Owen looked startled. "What do you mean?"

"Well, I suppose the bottom line is that Mum threw me out."

"What?! Why?"

"Because we weren't getting along," Anna replied as vaguely as possible.

"But there has to be more to it than that," prompted Owen.

"We were arguing. All the time. It got ridiculous. There were times when we wouldn't speak to each other for days on end. We'd cross paths in the hall and look through each other as though there was no one there. If the phone rang and Mum picked it up and it was for me, she'd hang up. And stupidly, I did the same."

"God, I knew you two didn't get along," Owen said, "but I can't believe Mum actually kicked you out."

"Oh, you wouldn't believe how grim it got,

even more so after you'd left home and gone to uni. We never really got on, you know that as much as I do. But while you were living at home, you managed to keep the peace between us; once you'd gone, we did nothing but fight."

"But the thing I still don't understand is why you didn't tell anyone where you were going. Especially me. I thought we were closer than that."

Anna struggled for something feasible to say. So far, she'd told nothing but the truth. She and her mum had been at each other's throats all the time; ultimately, though, that wasn't the only reason she'd left. If only it was that simple...

"I... uh, well, you see... there was also this guy..."

"Who?" Owen cut in. "Would I know him?"

"No, he was no one you knew, although you might have heard me mention him once or twice on the phone. Anyway, we'd been seeing each other for a while and it just wasn't working. I wanted to break it off with him, but he, uh, started to get difficult..."

"What the hell do you mean, Anna?" demanded Owen, looking agitated for the first time. "He didn't threaten you, did he? He didn't hit you? Who the heck *was* this guy?"

"No, no, none of those things," Anna said

and, choosing her words carefully, added, "he was never physically violent to me, but he was the type who could be, if you know what I mean. He was a bad sort and I guess I should have seen it coming. But I didn't. When I first met him, Mum and I were so much at loggerheads that it felt good to have someone being nice to me. I fell for him really quickly – dived straight in there without even thinking about it. Then, after a while, he started to show his true colours and that's when I realised I had to get away."

By now Owen was pacing the room, clearly disturbed by what he was hearing. "So what do you mean when you say he showed his true colours? What is it you're not telling me, Anna?"

If Anna wasn't careful, she knew she would end up revealing much more than she was prepared to. And she certainly didn't want to tell Owen the whole truth about David. Not yet.

"What I'm trying to say is that the guy was a mess. He had a dodgy past; he'd been in trouble with the police; he'd been expelled from school. He was bad news. Normally, I would have sussed someone like him out and steered well clear, but, like I said, I was feeling the need to be loved when I first met him."

She paused, searching for the right words. "The longer we went out the more I realised how

jealous he could be. He wanted to know my every move when I wasn't with him. And yes, actually, towards the end he *did* threaten me. That was when I knew I had to get away – before he hurt me."

"I can hardly believe what I'm hearing!" raged Owen. "Why on earth didn't you tell me when it was going on? I would have sorted him out!"

"I know," Anna said coolly. "And that's why I didn't tell you. It was my problem, not yours. I didn't want you steaming in and thumping David – I didn't want you to get involved, to fight my battles for me. I was the one who had to deal with it. So I left home and didn't tell anyone where I was going in case he tried to find me."

Owen slumped back down in a chair and ran his fingers through his hair. The muscles on his face were pulled tight – his whole expression a mask of tension. Anna could see his eyes flickering as his brain whirred, taking all the information in. She knew the grilling wasn't over yet.

"So did Mum know what was happening with this... this animal?"

"God, no! Like I said we were hardly speaking. And when things got bad between me and David I was hardly likely to go running to Mum with my problems, was I? That would have made me seem

like a total loser. No, I kept it to myself, just like I kept the bad stuff going on at home to myself. I figured I'd got myself into this mess and it was up to me to get myself out of it."

"So you ran away..."

"Yeah, at the time it seemed like the only way out."

"And you've got no regrets?"

Tons, Anna thought. *You don't know the half of it.* "Of course, I would have liked to have put you in the picture earlier rather than have you traipsing halfway across the country looking for me. But, like I said, the stuff with David was pretty heavy and – and – I guess, in a lot of ways, I was ashamed that I'd got involved with someone like him. That's why I wanted to sort it out by myself."

Anna went over to where her brother who had slumped in a chair and sat on the arm next to him. She put her arm round his shoulder and gave it a big squeeze.

"Telling you has lifted a huge weight off my mind," she said, trying to diffuse the situation a little. "And seeing you is the best thing that's happened to me in ages."

Owen took her hand in his and studied her face earnestly.

"You amaze me," he said. "It's like I'm meeting

you for the first time; you're a completely different person from the geeky kid I left at home. You've really grown up."

"Yeah, well, I guess I had to," smiled Anna ruefully. "But let's change the subject. I don't suppose there's any chance you can stay for a while? We've got so much to catch up on and I have been a bit of a sad old bag here on my own. It'd be great to have some company."

Owen smiled warmly at his sister and nodded enthusiastically. "Fortunately for you, we unemployed people get plenty of holidays, so yeah, I can stick around."

Anna threw her arms around Owen's neck and squeezed him so tightly he thought he'd explode. "That's brilliant!" she beamed. "You've made my year. I haven't got much room here but you're welcome to the sofa. And I'm sure I can scrounge a few days off from Nick if I sort it with him and Ollie. If not, you'll just have to be my kitchen hand for a while."

"I think I can cope with that," said Owen. "From where I was sitting today the view in the café looks pretty stunning, I'd say."

"Oh, yeah?" Anna grinned. "Who have you seen that you fancy?"

"I'm not sure I should say," he laughed. "You might warn her off me."

"It's more likely to be the other way round with some of the girls we get in the café," replied Anna. "So, come on, who is it?"

"OK, OK," he said, hands held up in a sign of defeat. "You're probably going to tell me that she's got a boyfriend, or is a raving lesbian, or has a huge personality disorder, or something..."

"Get on with it, will you?"

"All right! Her name's Sonja."

CHAPTER 12

● ●

MATT COMES UP TRUMPS

"I can't decide whether to ring him or not. I mean, it's been nearly two days now since he said he'd phone me and he hasn't."

Sonja and Kerry were walking towards the End on a fantastically warm morning. "And while I'd like to speak to him to see if he wants to meet up again," continued Sonja, "I don't want to appear too keen. What do you think?"

In a teeny-tiny cropped top and shorts, Sonja looked as if she was on holiday in Majorca; by contrast, Kerry felt quite overdressed in her jeans and deliberately bum-covering long shirt. As Sonja had already explained, her choice of outfit had been carefully contrived that morning.

"It's my get-Owen-to-notice-me look," she had said. "I spent most of last night in my wardrobe."

Miraculously, in contrast to a few days ago, her hormones seemed to be in tune with her again. Indulging fully in her current boy-obsessed mood, she had gone from explaining how she was dressing to please Owen to fretting over whether to call Kyle or not. And Kerry was finding it hard to keep up.

"Sorry, Son," Kerry frowned, "who are we talking about here? I've lost the plot a bit."

"Come on, Kez, I'm on about Kyle. What do you think I should do?"

Kerry didn't have a clue. She was finding it hard enough to get over the fact that Sonja was asking *her* advice on matters of a boy nature, rather than the other way round. Her mind flailing for a suitable answer, she suddenly hit on a valid solution.

"Have you thought that he might be thinking exactly the same as you?" she asked. "He might be desperate to call, but realises how uncool it is to call a girl you like so soon after a first date. 'Cause that's how their minds work, isn't it? So, if he really likes you, which I'm sure he does, he'll be dead chuffed if you call him."

Sonja turned to her friend, her eyes glinting with delight. "Of course, I hadn't thought of it like that. You're right. I'll call as soon as we get to the café."

"Uh, hang on. What about Owen? What if he's there?"

"That's an even more perfect solution," beamed Sonja. "If Owen's there, I won't need to call Kyle because I'll have my attention fully occupied with him. But if he isn't, why waste any more time worrying about what's right to do? I'll just pick up the phone and ring."

Kerry smiled inwardly. She was amazed how someone as stunning as her best friend could go from being unsure of herself one minute to brimming with confidence the next. As opposed to Kerry, who totally lacked faith in herself at all times. Granted, she had improved a bit since she'd started going out with Ollie, but not a great deal. And it didn't take much to knock her self-belief back to first base.

In the café, Kerry could see Matt, Ollie and Joe sitting in the window seat, with Maya and Catrina opposite. Ollie noticed them approaching first and gave Kerry a big smile and a wave which made her feel all funny and warm inside.

Sonja bounded in and scanned the room. "Hi, guys," she said, not looking at them at all but searching for Owen. But he wasn't there, so she sat down, disappointed that he hadn't seen her best assets walking in – her endlessly long, golden-tanned legs.

"Before you ask, we haven't seen him," Ollie grinned to Sonja as he got up and planted a kiss on Kerry's lips.

"What? Who?" Sonja asked, all innocent.

"Your latest love-god, that's who," added Matt. "Though Anna's in the kitchen cooking me a fry-up. I'll go and ask her where he is for you, if you like." He made as if to do just that.

"Sit down, you prat!" Sonja hissed. "Don't make it obvious."

"Pah!" Cat pretended to choke on her coffee. "Like as if what you're wearing isn't obvious enough."

"That's rich coming from someone who's sitting there in a spangly gold bikini top!" Sonja rattled back. "You look like you're ready to audition for some girlie dance group."

"If you can't be nice to each other, at least have the decency to spare the rest of us the bickering and shut up," interrupted Maya. "I might as well be back at home with my sister, listening to this."

"Sorry, Maya," said Sonja and bit her lip in an attempt not to laugh at Maya's outburst. "It was just a bit of gentle sparring. Honest."

At that moment Anna walked out of the kitchen carrying a full English breakfast which she brought over and put in front of Matt.

"There you go, Matt," she smiled, then turned

to the new arrivals. "Morning, Sonja, Kerry. Can I get you anything?"

"Coffee, please," Kerry replied.

"Make that two," added Sonja.

"Make it three. Please," said a voice from behind. Turning round, Anna saw her brother, looking the worse for wear.

"Hi, guys," he yawned. "Sorry, Anna, I guess I overslept. Must have been that red wine we drank last night." He looked at the plate of eggs, bacon, sausages and beans Matt was wolfing down. "Mmmm, that smells delicious. Any chance of a plateful for me?"

"Sure, no problem. Sit down and I'll bring it over."

"Thanks." He watched as she made her way back to the kitchen.

"Sit with us," offered Matt before Owen could wander off to another table. *Sonja will owe me one for this*, he thought.

"Are you sure?" Owen replied. "I'm not much company first thing in the morning, especially with a hangover. But if you don't mind..."

He slid into the banquette next to Matt and opposite Sonja, who hadn't taken her eyes off him ever since he'd walked in. He must have felt her eyes boring into him because he looked up at her and smiled.

"I meant to thank you for getting Anna for me yesterday," he said. "It was much appreciated."

"No problem," Sonja smiled back. "Glad to be of service. You two had a good night then?"

"Er, yeah, I think so. Although my insides might not agree with me at this present moment."

"Are you staying long?" Sonja asked.

"Yeah, I think I probably am," he replied. "I don't have anything else booked into my life at the moment so I might as well stick around for a few weeks. I'll see how it goes. I think Anna's got plans to turn me into her kitchen slave while I'm here, which will be interesting since my cooking's limited to chips and chilli."

"Don't worry, mate," Ollie broke in. "Mine's not much better and I work here."

Anna returned with a huge plate of fried food and three mugs of steaming coffee. Owen practically grabbed the plate out of her hand and began scoffing greedily, while Anna laughed and stood at the end of the table to watch him demolish it.

By this time Matt had finished his breakfast, which he let everyone know by letting out a loud burp of contentment. This, of course, repelled the girls who cried "Eurrrgh!" in unison and made the boys snigger. But it had the desired effect, which was to get everyone's attention.

"I thought I might have a bit of a bash at my place tomorrow night," he announced. "What do you think?"

"So long as you manage to keep your manners in check," replied Cat. "What's it in aid of?"

"Nothing. As usual. My old man's away on business again for a few days so I figured I'd make the most of a good opportunity. Nothing too flash, mind. I thought it could be just you lot – you and Owen too, Anna – maybe a few other people, a few beers and crisps and some good music. What do you say?"

Nice one, thought Sonia. *Well done, Matt. You're a real pal.*

CHAPTER 13

• •

SONJA ON A ROLL

Sonja took at least three hours to get ready for Matt's party. More if you counted the fact that, since she wanted to make a special effort for Owen, she'd spent ages earlier in the day deciding what to wear. And, of course, she'd been on the phone to Matt to thank him for doing his bit to help her in her bid to get together with Owen. And she'd called Ollie at the End to check that Anna (and more importantly Owen) were actually going too. Which they were.

The one person she hadn't phoned was Kyle. Now that she had a new guy in her sights, Sonja wasn't so bothered about contacting him. Instead, her thoughts were filled with imaginary scenes in which she snogged Owen.

She had been disappointed when he had said

he'd only be around for a few weeks; Sonja had hoped he was going to become a permanent fixture. But if that was all the time she had, so be it. At least she knew where she stood, which was more than could be said for the elusive Kyle.

Sonja was putting the finishing touches to her nails when the phone rang. Unwilling to pick it up in case she smudged her Nearly Nude polish, she left it for one of her family to answer. Then she heard her mum shouting that it was for her. *Darn!* Talk about inconvenient.

Waving her hands around frantically to dry her nails, she went over to the extension on her bedside table and gingerly picked up the receiver.

"Hello?" she said, a note of irritation in her voice.

"Sonja, hi. It's Kyle."

"Oh!" She couldn't contain the surprise in her voice – somehow he was the last person she was expecting to ring right now.

"Uh, how are you?" he asked. There was a note of reticence in his voice. But then perhaps he'd expected a more enthusiastic reception than 'Oh!' and then complete silence.

"I'm fine, thanks. How are you?" Sonja began frantically gathering her thoughts together so that they were in Kyle, rather than Owen, mode.

"I'm good. I was just calling to see if you

wanted to go out some time. I thought maybe we could go to a bar in the city or something."

"Yeah, great idea, I'd love to," enthused Sonja finally.

"How about Thursday?"

"Ooh, I can't Thursday or Friday," she lied, not wanting to appear too available. "How about Wednesday?"

"Sure, excellent. Actually Wednesday's better for me too. Shall I pick you up... at eight o'clock, maybe?"

"Good idea."

"OK, well I'll see you then..."

"Yeah, OK. It'll be fun."

"Bye then."

"Bye, Kyle."

Sonja put the phone down and did a little jig of delight around her room.

• • •

As Owen and Anna walked up the lane towards Matt's on the posh side of town, they could hear the thumping bass of his sound system well before they even saw the house.

"If the noise is anything to go by, it sounds good," commented Owen.

"Yeah, well, Matt certainly likes to party,"

Anna replied. "He's always having people round, so I hear."

"You haven't actually been round yourself before now then?"

"No. To be honest I've never been invited. And even if I had, I would have made an excuse not to go. I would have done the same tonight if you hadn't been here. I'm not sure all this is my scene any more."

"Rubbish!" her brother scoffed. "You were always out partying when you lived at home..."

"Yeah, talk about too much too young..." she sighed and was silent for a moment. "Anyway, I'm here now." She touched Owen's sleeve and put her arm through his. "And I'm up for a good time. And no doubt Sonja will be here too, so you'll have your hands full all evening. If you're really lucky."

"Yeah, I *wish*."

They were at the front door now, so Anna reached up and rang the bell and banged the goblin-headed door knocker for good measure. Soon Matt was standing in front of them, summoning them in and leading them off in the direction of his den and the back garden beyond.

"I'm just sorting out some more tracks to play," he shouted above the noise. "Help yourself to booze. You'll find everyone in the garden."

Owen pulled eight cans of lager from the carrier he was holding and put them on a table. He took one for himself and handed another to Anna, then they went into the garden which was lit with outdoor candles and a strobe light coming from the house.

Seeing Ollie, Kerry and Sonja sitting under a tree together, they went over.

"You made it then," Ollie shouted cheerfully when he saw them.

"Yeah," Anna replied. "The café was empty by eight thirty so we'd cleaned up and were ready to close on the stroke of nine. How's the party going?"

"Loudly. Sit down."

Noticing that Owen had already plonked himself next to Sonja and was laughing at something she'd said, Anna sat opposite Ollie and Kerry and took a gulp of lager. It was warm and bitter and deeply unpleasant – not the sort of drink she'd normally touch – but she thought it would ease her nerves a little so she forced it down.

"It's good to see you outside work for a change," enthused Ollie. "You must sometimes wonder if there's any life beyond Nick's kitchen."

Anna smiled. "I don't mind it actually, I like keeping busy. And it's a nice place to work."

"Yeah, Uncle Nick's all right, isn't he?" Ollie said.

"Everyone is. You've all been really nice to me since I moved in," Anna beamed, taking another sip of lager. "I'm really happy here, I'm beginning to feel like I've lived here all my life, not just a few months."

"The café sometimes has that effect on you," laughed Ollie. "It's a bit like living in a time warp: if you're not careful, you get completely sucked in and start dreaming about burgers and chips."

"I already do!" laughed Anna.

"Which is why you need to get out and about more. I'm glad you decided to come here tonight; you'll have to come out with us again."

"Thanks," Anna grinned, "I will. Actually, I expect Owen will be dragging me out once or twice while he's here."

"He seems ever so nice," said Kerry, looking over to where Owen was engrossed in conversation with Sonja.

"He is, he's brilliant. We're really close."

"You're lucky," Kerry said. "I'm close to my brother, but he's only a kid. You can't share too many secrets with a six-year-old."

Anna smile wryly. "I don't know that we share secrets, but he's always acted as a buffer between me and Mum."

"Oh," Kerry said. "Don't you get on with your mum?"

"Not really. We rub each other up the wrong way. When Owen lived at home, he was always the mediator. Otherwise, we would probably have killed each other."

"So what happened when he left home?"

"We nearly killed each other!" Anna laughed. "In the end, I left."

It was the most candid she'd been with anyone since she'd arrived in Winstead, and she found it a lot easier opening up than she'd expected. *Talking to Owen the other night must have helped*, she thought.

Over the next couple of hours she found herself telling Kerry and Ollie more about herself than she'd ever imagined.

By the end of the night, Anna had really begun to let her hair down. She'd chatted to everyone, given it loads on the makeshift dancefloor/patio, and she'd even had a light-hearted smooch with Matt. She'd also drunk two cans of lager and was feeling very light-headed by the end of it.

She had hardly spoken to Owen all evening, which was a surprise to her since she'd assumed she would feel the need to cling to him for support to help her get through the party which she'd been slightly dreading.

Although she felt she knew the gang on a superficial level, they were all such great friends she wasn't sure about butting in on their clique like this – however much they seemed to want her company.

As it was, she hadn't needed Owen at all, which was a good thing since he and Sonja seemed to have commandeered each other's attention for the entire evening.

When, much later on, she realised that most people had gone home and only she and Matt were left, Anna decided it really was time to go. But as she looked for Owen, it dawned on her that she hadn't seen him for a good hour or so. Or Sonja. Surely he wouldn't have left without her?

Anna searched the garden, then went inside the house and began hunting through the downstairs rooms. Where the heck was he?

And then she saw them. Standing in a dark recess in the dining room, Owen and Sonja were wrapped around each other, snogging furiously.

CHAPTER 14

● ●

THE MISSING PIECES

Sonja's life suddenly felt like a giddy whirl of activity. From having no interest in guys for months, suddenly here she was with two on the go at once.

"And they're both such a laugh, and exciting, and so different... and such good snoggers, if you know what I mean," she told Kerry gleefully on the phone the following night.

"Yes, Ollie told me all about the tonsil tennis you were playing with Owen," Kerry replied. "Anna couldn't wait to tell him about how she'd walked in on you both at Matt's. She said she thought she was more embarrassed than the two of you put together."

"She did look a bit put out." Sonja's eyes glittered at the memory. "Owen said she'd

probably never seen her big brother snogging anyone before."

"So when are you seeing him again?"

"Friday night. He's taking me for a meal. I can't wait."

"I think it's great that you've hit it off together," said Kerry, "but doesn't it bother you that he's only likely to be here for a short time?"

"Yes and no," Sonja reasoned. "Yeah, it'd be lovely to think he lived here, you know, to see what develops. But on the other hand, at least I'm aware that it's going to end, so there's no point getting involved in a big way. It's a bit like a holiday romance, you know? You enjoy it while it lasts but have no illusions that anything's going to come of it afterwards."

"And, of course, there's always Kyle to fall back on once it's over," added Kerry wryly.

"I guess so." Sonja was silent for a moment. "I hadn't thought of it like that. But, yeah, in a lot of ways that'll soften the blow. That sounds really calculating, doesn't it?"

"Well, you weren't to know it was going to happen like this, were you?"

"No. But you and Ollie haven't said anything to Anna about Kyle, have you? Only Owen asked me if I had a boyfriend last night and I said no."

"No, we haven't said a word. Wouldn't dream

of it. Anyway, it's not as if you and Kyle are an item yet..."

"No, not after one date. We might break up the next time I see him."

"Which is when?"

"Tomorrow night."

"God, I can hardly keep up!" Kerry laughed down the phone. "Don't forget we're supposed to be going out one night together, too, will you?"

"No. Shall we do something together on Saturday? Maybe go clubbing?"

"Sure, so long as you haven't got a string of other guys lined up to take you out somewhere by then. I don't want to cramp your style, not while you're on a roll."

"Don't worry, you won't. I might even pass on a few stray crumbs to you, if you're really lucky."

"Eurrgh! Spare me, please."

• • •

"Doesn't it bother you that you're not here for long? I mean, it's not as though this is going to be a big romance, is it? If it was me, I'd wonder what the point was."

Anna lay sprawled on the sofa in her living room and watched Owen cooking chilli for dinner in the kitchen area. After an afternoon spent

having a lazy picnic by the river (while Joe had obligingly taken over her shift at the café), she was now quizzing Owen on her favourite subject of the moment: Sonja.

Owen grabbed a tea towel and threw it at her. "I can't believe you're such a misery guts!" he laughed. "Haven't you heard of spontaneity, of living for the moment? We're just having a bit of fun. Where's the harm in that?"

"None, so long as you both know where you stand."

"Which we do. Sonja knows I'm going back to Manchester soon. We're just having a good time while it lasts."

"You don't worry that she might fall for you big time?"

"I think it's more likely to be the other way round, if anything," admitted Owen, a touch ruefully. "She's such a great person and a real laugh."

"And devastatingly attractive."

"I know, it does help. And single too – that's what I can't understand. I was amazed when I asked her if she had a boyfriend and she said no. Unbelievable!"

"From what I can gather she gets a lot of interest, but she turns most of them down. She must be quite fussy. So quite what she's doing with you, God only knows."

"Cheers, sis. Thanks for the vote of confidence."

"Any time. So when are you seeing her again?"

"We're going for something to eat on Friday night. Got any ideas where I can take her?"

"Well, there's this lovely cheap café I know only a stone's throw from here..."

"Yeah, that'd really impress her, wouldn't it?" he guffawed. "She'd think I was a right old cheapskate. And I'm sure she'd be dead chuffed to share the evening with all her mates, too..."

"Actually, I *have* heard of somewhere. There's a little Italian restaurant off the High Street. It's supposed to be not too expensive, but nice and intimate and romantic. It's called Luigi's, I think."

"Great. I'll suggest we go there."

"So if you lived nearer, would you want to see Sonja on a more serious basis?"

"Yeah, definitely, if she'd let me. But there's no point in going down that road because it's not likely to happen. Live for today, that's my motto at the moment."

"Well, you're certainly doing that."

Seeing that dinner was almost ready, Anna got up and began gathering plates and cutlery for their meal. She loved having Owen around. It was nice to have someone to chat to and share a meal with in the evenings.

She was beginning to feel as though she was living again, rather than just existing from one day to the next. The only problem was that she was already beginning to dread the thought of him leaving.

"Have you got anything planned for tomorrow?" she asked as Owen dished up the food. "Because you can always help me out in the kitchen if you're stuck for something to do."

"I will if you like," he said. "But one thing I had thought of doing was phoning Mum to see if she fancied a day out in Winstead in the next week or so."

"What?!" Anna was so shocked she nearly dropped the plates she was carrying to the table.

"Well, I thought it would be a good opportunity for you two to talk, to maybe resolve your differences."

Anna looked panic-stricken. "Oh, no! There's no way!" she wailed, slumping down on to the sofa, her head in her hands. She couldn't cope with seeing her mum again, not after everything that had happened between them.

Owen just didn't seem to understand. But then maybe he couldn't as she hadn't told him the full story.

Anna's mind raced. Maybe she owed it to Owen to put him completely in the picture. He

was her brother after all, and she'd missed him so much since she'd been away. Perhaps it was time to let him in.

"I... uh, don't know how..." She stumbled over her words, searching for a way to begin. "Look, I'm not ready to see Mum yet."

"Why not?"

"Because I haven't told you everything."

"What do you mean?" Owen asked.

"I mean, there's more... stuff, that you don't know about."

"Like what?"

"Like how the biggest reason I left home was because I had an abortion, and afterwards I couldn't bear to stay."

Anna felt the words tumble out of her mouth all too quickly. Then she looked into her brother's eyes and waited for his reaction. Complete shock.

"Jesus!" he exclaimed. "You did *what*?"

"I had an abortion," Anna repeated quietly. She took a deep breath before speaking again.

"What I'm trying to tell you is that yes, all those reasons I gave you for leaving home the other day are absolutely true. But the biggest thing... the main reason for going was because I got pregnant and then got rid of the baby."

Owen looked incredulous, as if he couldn't take in what he was hearing.

"Go on," he muttered.

"Oh, it was awful, Owen. Mum was so angry about the pregnancy – I was only just seventeen, for God's sake – but I really thought she'd get over that and be supportive. Which was what I desperately needed. But she didn't, she totally lost it. She said getting pregnant would ruin my life, that I'd have no future. She said I was too young to look after a baby and that once I realised what I'd done and that I'd thrown my life away, then I'd dump it on her to look after. And that would ruin her life too."

Anna gulped a little before continuing. "And deep down I knew part of what she said was right. I would have been throwing away my life or at least a large part of it. And although I fleetingly toyed with the idea of keeping the baby, I knew it wasn't an option for me. Not really. It was a stupid mistake, one which I'd regret for the rest of my life. But it was a mistake I could rectify, to a certain extent."

She paused again, then looked her brother straight in the eyes. "So, after I'd agonised for a few days, and talked to our doctor about it, I told Mum I was going to have an abortion. I thought she'd be relieved…"

"Jesus, Anna, she tried to bring us up as Catholics! You know what she thinks about

abortion. You must have known how she'd react...?"

"I suppose so. But I wasn't thinking straight. I was scared. I needed her help – I was crying out for some support. She went totally off the rails and chucked all this stuff about God in to make me feel guilty. About how having an abortion was totally against our religion. About how I was a sinner and how she wouldn't be able to go back to church if I went through with it and aborted the baby."

Anna fought back the tears that were pricking at the back of her eyes. "She told me it would ruin *her* life as well as my own because God would never forgive us. She seemed most concerned for herself – that God would never forgive her if she let me go through with it."

Reliving the pain she had felt made Anna shoot out of her seat and start pacing the room.

"That made me so angry – how dare she tell me I was ruining her life? That was so selfish of her. She was palming her religious feelings of guilt off on me. I just flipped and said some things that maybe I shouldn't. That's when she told me she couldn't live under the same roof as someone who was 'blaspheming against God' as she put it. Oh Owen, I wanted to leave that day, but what could I do?"

Owen shook his head in sympathy. "Go on," he encouraged.

"I'd got an appointment with the hospital consultant. I needed to keep it. So I went on my own, though I wished I had somebody with me. I was terrified. Anyway, he agreed with my doctor that the termination should go ahead and I went into hospital ten days later..."

Anna's voice dropped to a whisper so that Owen could barely hear her.

"...That's it really. I stayed at home for a few days after the operation, but I just couldn't bear the terrible atmosphere in the house... Mum's recrimination... So one day, while she was out, I simply packed my bags and left."

"And you haven't been in touch with each other since?"

"No."

Anna glanced at her brother. Seeing the look of pity on his face was enough to make a lakeful of tears well up in her eyes.

Owen came over and gave her a big, comforting hug.

"Oh, Anna, I'm so sorry," he said, his chin resting on the top of her head, a look of consternation on his face. "I *knew* there was something you weren't telling me the other day, I could feel you were holding back, but I hadn't a

clue *what*. You poor thing, you've really been through it, haven't you?"

Anna found a tissue and tried to wipe away some of the tears.

"It was awful. Making that appointment to see my doctor was one of the loneliest things I've ever done," she whispered. "Fortunately, she was kind and understanding. She arranged the consultation at the hospital for me. Then she offered me counselling when she realised that I was alone, but I refused. I just wanted it to be all over."

She paused for a moment. "But it's not over. I felt absolutely terrible afterwards. I still do. It was the hardest thing I've ever had to do; probably will be too. I know I'll never forget it. But I was barely seventeen. I couldn't bring a child into the world when I still felt like one myself. It wouldn't have been fair, on either of us."

"But what about the father...?" Owen sighed. "I suppose you're going to tell me it was that David."

"Yep. 'Fraid so. And that was my other big mistake. Telling him, I mean. Because by this time the cracks were beginning to show in our relationship. Once I found out I was pregnant, I stupidly and naively got it into my head that a baby could make things better between us. *That's* how dumb I was."

Anna sat down again, suddenly feeling exhausted. "But when I told David, he didn't want to know. That's when I realised what a complete and utter sod he was. He didn't want to have a baby with me. What I couldn't cope with was that *he* didn't want me to have an abortion either."

Looking at her brother's outraged expression, Anna gave a bitter smile.

"I guess he quite liked the idea of fathering a child, so long as there were no strings attached. And preferably no maintenance charges. David made it obvious that if I had the baby, I was going to be on my own. Then, when I told him I was definitely having an abortion, he threatened to kill me; said he'd come looking for me and make sure I paid for what I'd done. It was another reason for leaving home. I didn't feel safe any more."

"I can't believe it! How could he be like that? You must have been so strong to have coped with it all."

"Possibly. But my overriding feeling was that there was no one I could trust, no one I could turn to for support. So I just had to go it alone. I felt like the only person left I could rely on was myself. That's what I've been doing ever since, and you know what? For me it works."

Anna sat back in her chair, the tension ebbing

from her body. The relief at telling someone was indescribable. She felt as if a huge weight had been lifted from her.

However, there were still some things she needed to say. By talking to Owen her jumbled thoughts and feelings of the last year were beginning to slot into place.

Maybe I should have gone for counselling, like the doctor suggested all those months ago, Anna thought ruefully.

"You know, at some point in the future I'd love to have a baby, but I want the circumstances to be right. I want to be settled and in a relationship, financially secure so that we could give it anything it wanted..."

Her voice trailed off and she looked up at Owen with the saddest expression in her eyes he had ever seen. He could feel his heart aching for her.

"Go on," he said gently.

"When I found out I was pregnant I had all these dreadful visions flashing through my mind. You know, of me being a single mum living off the state in a grotty council flat with no money and no future. I didn't want that sort of life for my child. Not if I could possibly avoid it.

"I realise that some girls my age don't feel they have the choice; they get stuck in a situation and

before they know it, it's too late to do anything about it. Or they might decide to have the baby, whatever the consequences. But I felt I had the right to choose, and I knew that if I could possibly avoid that kind of life, then I would."

Anna watched her brother for his reaction. Owen said nothing for a while. He was mulling over Anna's astounding revelations. Anna valued his viewpoint on life so much and she was curious – even a little frightened – as to what he might say next.

"You know," he finally sighed, "I'm staggered by what you've told me. You've been through so much on your own. And I can understand you wanting this David guy out of your life. He was obviously a big mistake from start to finish. But Mum too?"

Owen paused again, searching for the right words.

"Surely, all the years of your life with her have meant something to you? To both of you? Of all the terrible things that have happened to you over the past year or so, surely your relationship with her is the one thing that you might be able to salvage from all this?"

"I know," replied Anna. "But a big part of me is still angry at her for not seeing it from my point of view and for not finding it in herself to be there

for me when I needed her most. That's what I find hard to forgive."

"I can understand that. But I bet she regrets what's happened as much as you do, if not more."

Anna laughed bitterly. "So why isn't she here having a conversation with me? Why is it you? Come on, Owen, it's always been left to you to make amends between Mum and me..."

"And that's as much down to your stubbornness as hers," her brother cut in, a little defensively.

"I'm not saying it isn't. But the fact of the matter is this: if she cared so much, if she's as remorseful as you think she is, why hasn't she confided in you? Put you in the picture? Asked for your help sorting this out?"

Owen didn't answer.

"Well, I'll tell you why, shall I?" Anna bristled. "It's because she wants to sweep this whole damn thing under the carpet and get on with her life, pretending it didn't happen. She's as bad as David, if not worse. She put me in an impossible situation, telling me I couldn't keep the baby but I couldn't have an abortion either. I can't tell you how bitter I feel towards her for that."

The chilli that Owen had spent time and effort preparing had gone cold and congealed in the time that they'd been talking. Neither of them

could face it now. Anna took the plates back to the kitchen and threw away the sorry-looking mess of food.

"I'm sorry, Owen," she said shaking. "Mum hurt me very badly. I'm not ready to face her yet – and I don't know if I ever will be."

CHAPTER 15

● ●

A HANDFUL OF TROUBLE

Sonja spent most of Wednesday trying to remember everything she had ever said to Kyle. She wasn't used to this two-timing lark and was a bit unsure as to whether she could keep the two boys' identities completely separate. She didn't want to start asking Kyle about how Manchester United were expected to do in the Cup this next season when in fact they were Owen's favourite team and Kyle supported Newcastle.

Nor did she want to assume that Kyle knew something about her when in fact she had spoken to Owen about it instead. By the time Kyle turned up on her doorstep ten minutes late, Sonja still wasn't confident she was going to get through the date without making more than one gaffe.

Kyle stood at the front door grinning from ear

to ear. He looked her up and, down and with great appreciation in his voice, announced, "You look nice. Who's the lucky guy?"

Sonja laughed and followed him down the path to the ancient-looking beige Ford Escort parked outside the house. She found she couldn't take her eyes off his seriously cute bum, the shape of which she could just make out as he walked.

Opening the passenger side door in what Sonja thought to be a very chivalrous gesture, he then climbed in himself and wriggled across to the driver's seat.

"Got a bit of a dodgy door my side," he explained. "If I open it, it might fall off all together. Come on, hop in."

Sonja wasn't entirely sure she wanted to 'hop in' a car that looked as if it might disintegrate once it hit twenty miles an hour.

On the other hand, she didn't want to appear like a nervous, ageing great auntie, so she grudgingly clambered in and quickly secured herself with the seat belt.

"So, Madam, where would you like me to take you this evening?" said Kyle in his best James the Chauffeur voice.

"To the most expensive bar in the city, please," she laughed.

"I know that was the plan," he chuckled, "but

I'm not convinced this old heap will get us there and back in one piece, if you know what I mean."

Sonja gave a hollow laugh. She was beginning to feel increasingly nervous about the evening. Part of her wished she was tucked up in a cosy restaurant with Owen. While the rest of her relished the thrill of not quite knowing where she was going to end up (and whether she would live to tell the tale).

"Oh, right," she said, trying to remain looking cool. "Well, we could always drive into the next town, see what sort of nightlife they've got to offer as competition for Winstead."

"OK, sure. There's a wild place I know that I've been to a couple of times before with the lads. It can get a bit rough at the end of the evening, but you'll be OK so long as you stick with me."

Oh, God, Sonja thought – not for the first time – *what am I letting myself in for here?* "Great," she managed cheerily, "whatever you fancy."

"That comes later," joked Kyle as he started the engine and sped off down the road. Or at least, Sonja hoped he was only joking.

When Kyle pulled into the neon-lit Smokin' Joe's situated on an industrial estate in the next town, Sonja knew she was in for a night to remember. When they walked through the door into a cigarette smoke-filled barn of a place with

wall to wall pool tables, she contemplated walking right back out again.

And when Kyle seemed to know everyone there – he even had his own cue behind the bar – she was pretty certain this whole thing had been planned. This was confirmed when she heard someone shout to Kyle, "'Bout time you showed your face, mate – you're up next."

She turned to Kyle, a frosty look on her face. "You were going to bring me here all along, weren't you? You had no intention of taking me on a proper date."

"I did, I promise you," he cried. "It's just that a spare slot came up in this pool tournament and I really wanted to play. But I didn't want to disappoint you either. So I figured that seeing as you're such a laugh and so cool, well, you wouldn't mind coming here. You're not angry, are you?"

Sonja knew that she had every right to be *very* angry but... what the hell, she'd never been anywhere quite like this before. The place was teeming with cute guys. And she knew it would be a great story to tell the others in the days to come.

"No, but this had better be worth my while," she said, feigning annoyance. She didn't want Kyle to relax just yet.

Secretly, of course, Sonja was in her element. She knew she looked good tonight and she caused a real stir as they walked to Kyle's allocated table. Unknown to Kyle, Sonja was a pretty hot pool player, so when he got knocked out in the first round of the tournament, she spent the rest of the evening thrashing him at pool as well. By the end of the night he was insisting that the balls on the table were rigged.

"You should have said you could play," he joked at one point. "I would have brought you here last time if I'd known."

"But then I would have missed out on Fat Larry's," smirked Sonja. "I'll say one thing for you, Kyle, you really know how to show a girl a classy time."

"Last of the big spenders, me," he grinned, getting the joke straightaway. Then he came over and put his arm around her waist and gave her a little butterfly kiss just below the ear lobe. Sonja melted. By the time they left, she was liking Kyle more and more.

"I've had a really good time," she said as they roared along the road back towards Winstead.

"Yeah, me too," he replied. "And my mates thought you were dead cool. In fact, I don't want the night to end yet. Shall we stop for a while and talk some more?"

Before Sonja could answer, he had veered left and was heading towards a lay-by at the side of the road.

"Why do you want to stop in a grotty dark lay-by full of litter?" Sonja asked coldly. "What exactly have you got in mind, Kyle? Whatever it is, you can forget it!"

Kyle obediently steered the car back on to the road and began chuckling out loud.

"What's so funny?" demanded Sonja, arms folded defensively across her chest.

"You," he laughed. "You don't miss a trick do you? Honest, I only wanted to stop for a wee."

"Phthtt!" Sonja spluttered in disbelief. "I'm not falling for that one. You must think I was born yesterday!" Inside, she was laughing her head off. *He's like a naughty schoolboy trying his luck*, she thought. *One who is all mouth but with nothing of substance to back it up*.

While she attempted to stifle her sniggers, Kyle tried to make amends. "I only wanted to talk. I wasn't going to try it on. I'd be too scared, especially after last time."

Grinning, he reaching across with his left hand and gently tapped her on the nose.

"Let me make it up to you. Let me take you somewhere really special and romantic, somewhere you've never been before. We'll go off

somewhere dead flash. Go on – what do you say?"

"Where are you planning on taking me?" Sonja asked, still trying not to laugh. "Greyhound racing? For pie and mash and mushy peas at the local chippy? Or maybe a slap-up take away pizza at your place?"

"Wherever, Son, wherever you like," he answered. "You choose. Just give me one more chance. Please."

"OK," Sonja relented. "One more chance. But any more tricks like this and you're out!"

CHAPTER 16

• •

THE TIME OF HER LIFE?

"I wonder how Sonja got on with Kyle the other night?" Maya mused to Kerry over Cokes at the End early on Friday evening. Then she wondered what she'd said as Kerry grabbed her arm and gave her a look of complete panic.

"What?" Maya whispered, both hands over her mouth and a shocked expression on her face. "What did I say?"

"Not so loud," hissed Kerry. "You don't want Anna to hear."

"Why not?" Maya was confused. "What's it got to do with her?"

"Well, for a start she'll tell Owen, and he'll probably get the hump because Son told him she wasn't going out with anyone, and then she'll be in big trouble." Kerry looked at Maya as though

129

she had completely lost the plot for not realising this.

Then it dawned on her that perhaps Maya wasn't fully aware of the Owen/Sonja/Kyle lust triangle. This was confirmed moments later.

"I don't know what you're talking about!"

"No, of course you don't," Kerry replied, her eyes like saucers and ready to pass on a good bit of gossip. "You weren't at Matt's on Monday, were you?"

"No, thanks to having to babysit my delightful brother and sister. I haven't seen any of you guys all week. So what happened?"

"Sonja got off with Owen."

"No! *Really*?"

"Yes, really. I mean, it was fairly inevitable. It was obvious they fancied the pants off each other right from the start. It was only a matter of time."

"So are they an item?"

Kerry nodded. "They're going out tonight. They're meeting here then going for a meal. Sonja said she'd try and get here early so we could catch up on what's been happening."

Maya still looked thoroughly bewildered by what she was hearing. "So does that mean she and Kyle are finished?"

"No, that's the thing. They went out on Wednesday night too, that's why she wants to

get here before Owen, so she can fill me in on the gory details."

Finally, the penny dropped. "So she's going out with both of them at the same time?" gasped Maya.

"Yeah," Kerry giggled. "She's really going for it at the moment. Having the time of her life."

Maya did not look amused. "So Owen doesn't know about Kyle, but does Kyle know about Owen?"

Kerry shook her head. "I wouldn't have thought so." She broke off and looked out of the window, down the road. "You can ask her yourself now. She's just coming."

Sonja breezed into the café in white knee-length boots, a pink miniskirt and duck-egg blue knitted top and matching cardigan.

"You look fabulous," Kerry said appreciatively.

"Thanks," Sonja replied, sitting down and taking a sip of Kerry's Coke. "You haven't seen Owen yet?" she said, glancing furtively around the bustling café.

"No sign of him."

"Good." Sonja leaned towards Kerry and Maya and took them on a graphic journey of her date with Kyle.

Kerry sat with her hand stuffed in her mouth to stifle her laughter for most of the time, while

even the disapproving Maya couldn't help letting out the odd giggle at Kyle's antics.

"The guy is unreal," Kerry spluttered when Sonja had finished. "He's so cheeky. He sounds like he needs a good slap."

"He gets a verbal slap every time I see him," Sonja countered. "But the thing is, I can't help liking him. He just cracks me up. And when I do shout at him to keep his hands to himself, he does. And then he's so meek and mild and full of remorse, I end up liking him all the more."

"So does Kyle know about Owen?" asked Maya pointedly.

"Christ, no," Sonja replied. "And Owen doesn't know about Kyle either, so please don't drop me in it, Maya."

"Sonja, I can't believe what you're doing," Maya said. "You've only been seeing these guys for a week – if that – and already you're lying to both of them. Imagine how *you* would feel if someone was doing it to you. You'd be livid, wouldn't you?"

The smile fell from Sonja's face. She shifted uncomfortably in her seat and picked at an imaginary bobble of fluff on her cardie.

"Well, I... uh..." she began.

She hadn't expected such a pointed question from her friend.

Indeed, what Maya was saying hadn't even crossed Sonja's mind. Not once.

"Yes, you're right, I guess I probably would be," she said finally. "But I didn't mean any of this to happen. I never expected to meet two guys that I liked in the space of a week, not in a million years. It just happened."

"So is that what you'll say when one of them finds out about the other? Would you accept that as a reason if the boot was on the other foot?"

Sonja didn't answer.

"Look, I'm not trying to have a go," Maya relented. "I'm just putting the other side of the story. And suggesting you should think about what you're doing. Ask yourself if you'd like the same thing done to you."

"To be fair to Sonja," Kerry came to her friend's rescue, "Owen's only going to be around for a few weeks, if that. He knows they're not likely to see each other again once he goes back home. I bet it wouldn't bother him too much if he found out."

"Well, why doesn't she tell him then?" insisted Maya.

"Quick everyone, change the subject," Kerry said hurriedly as she looked up and saw Owen heading their way. "He's coming. So Sonja," she added, frantically thinking of a change of subject,

"don't forget our night out tomorrow. Where d'you fancy going?"

Sonja was clearly mulling over Maya's words of warning. She only managed to say, "Uh, I dunno. You choose," before Owen was upon them.

"Hi, guys," he said cheerfully. "How's it going?"

Kerry smiled and managed a cheery 'hello', while Maya looked guilt-ridden and as though she'd rather be somewhere else. Sonja stood up and slid out of the banquette.

"Wow, you look amazing, Sonja," enthused Owen as she stood up to her full height in front of him.

Sonja gave him a humble smile, said a vague 'bye' to the others, and walked out of the café.

• • •

"You seem a bit subdued, Son. Is everything OK?"

Sonja smoothed the red and white check napkin that was lying across her lap and began fiddling uneasily with her bread knife. She had hardly said a word since she and Owen had left the End.

She had been worrying and fretting over what Maya had said to the point that it had become a huge issue in her head. Instead of concentrating

on having a good time at Luigi's with Owen, she was wondering whether she should come clean about Kyle.

She knew Maya had a point; Sonja wouldn't tolerate being lied to by a guy, however new the relationship. But how many people start going out together knowing that they're only going to last a couple of weeks? Not many. That was why her situation was unusual, and that was why she had so far bottled out of confessing to Owen this evening. Now, halfway through their starters in the cutely romantic restaurant she had wanted to come to with Kyle, she still couldn't bring herself to say anything.

"Everything's great," Sonja answered, suddenly realising she must seem like a complete misery. "Really. And this restaurant is lovely. I've been wanting to come here for ages – I just haven't been in the right company."

She smiled to herself. Owen and Kyle might easily have come from opposite ends of the universe – they were so different. She doubted whether Kyle had a speck of romance in his entire body, whereas Owen found it the most natural thing in the world to bring a date somewhere as intimate as this. And she couldn't ever imagine Kyle noticing if she was 'subdued' – he'd be too busy trying it on with her.

"You know, I can't believe you haven't got loads of guys after you," said Owen. "You'd have them queuing down the road if you lived in Manchester..."

This was it – the perfect opportunity for Sonja to admit that she was seeing someone else. But before she could open her mouth to speak, Owen was talking again.

"It's a shame you don't live there, or me here, because I'd be first in the queue to snap you up. Instead, I'm stuck with a holiday romance that I wish would never come to an end."

He leaned across the table and took hold of her hand.

It was such a lovely moment and he was obviously waiting for her to say something. She couldn't mention Kyle now. He'd already made it obvious that what they were experiencing together had a very limited shelf-life. What was the point in spoiling it?

"I know," she said. "I feel the same way. But at least we can have a good time together while you're here, and who's to say you might not visit Anna again sometime? Or I might even take a trip up to where you live one day."

"If I believed that there wasn't some guy you're going to fall for waiting around the corner, I would cling on to a thought like that," said Owen.

"As it is, I bet you'll have forgotten about me in a couple of weeks."

"I could say the same about you."

"No. I won't forget you in a hurry, Son. You're a very special person who will one day make some incredibly lucky guy very happy."

Sonja thought that was the nicest thing anyone had ever said to her.

CHAPTER 17

DOUBLE TROUBLE FOR SONJA

"You don't mind me going out with Sonja, do you? I mean, after all that stuff about me neglecting her, I thought we ought to do something together, just the two of us."

Kerry sat on a bar stool at The Swan, Ollie's parents' pub, and fretted over the fact that she had agreed to spend Saturday night clubbing with Sonja rather than with Ollie (who, if she was being honest, she would rather be with).

"Stop worrying," Ollie said and gave her an affectionate squeeze on the hand. "Go out and enjoy yourselves; do whatever it is you girls get up to on your nights out. And anyway, we're seeing each other now, even if it's only while you wait for Sonja to turn up."

Normally, Sonja and Kerry would have got

ready to go out together, but Kerry had opted to go for a quiet drink with Ollie first.

Kerry took a sip from her glass and sighed. "It's amazing to think how much has happened since she and I had that conversation about me spending so much time with you and not enough with her. Who would have thought that Sonja would have two guys on the boil so soon after?"

"I know."

"Are you seeing Joe tonight?" Kerry asked.

"He said he'd call in. We've been talking about getting the band going again and he seems really enthusiastic. We've got loads to sort out, I only hope something comes of it this time."

Ollie looked over Kerry's shoulder and saw Sonja rush in. She came whizzing over at breakneck speed.

"Sorry I'm late, Kez," she hollered. "I completely lost track of time. Dad's outside in the car – he gave me a lift here and he'll take us round to Enigma if we go now. Hi, Ol. Bye, Ol." And with that she turned and disappeared back out of the pub.

Kerry slid off her stool, gave Ollie a quick goodnight kiss and ran after her friend.

"So how did it go with Owen last night?" Kerry demanded once Sonja's father had dropped them off.

"Nice, really nice," Sonja swooned. "I can't believe he's not going to be around for long. It's so unfair!"

"Well, maybe you could work something out between you so that you still get to see each other," suggested Kerry helpfully.

"I don't think so. He's already made it plain that nothing's going to happen long term, and it's not practical, I can see that as much as him. And anyway, Maya had a point – it's not nice to be carrying on with two guys at once. I can see it now."

"She could have been a bit more subtle about it."

"I guess so. But any less subtle and I might not have taken the hint."

"So does that mean you told Owen about Kyle?" Kerry asked, intrigued.

"No, but I thought about it, which is more than I have done up until now." Sonja gave a hollow little laugh as they joined the queue of clubbers waiting to get into Enigma.

They paid their entrance fees and went inside. Squeezing past an already heaving throng of bodies they made their way to the toilets to make sure their make-up hadn't slipped since they'd left home.

Reassured after much tweaking in front of the deeply unflattering neon wall mirrors, they finally

came out and picked their way towards one of the two dance floors.

Sonja suddenly stopped dead. "Oh, my God!" she cried. "Kyle!"

Straight in front of them, and heading their way, was indeed Kyle. He spotted Sonja a split second after she'd spotted him and he looked as shocked as she did.

"Hi there," Sonja shouted cheerfully, not entirely sure whether she was pleased to see him or not. "Fancy seeing you here."

"Yeah, fancy," came the equally unsure reply. "Er, I didn't know you came here."

"We don't. Usually." Sonja motioned to Kerry. "We're having a night out, just the two of us, and we thought we'd come here for a change."

"Great," Kyle answered. "Well, why don't I buy you both a drink? What'll it be?"

Their orders taken, he sidled off to the bar, leaving Sonja feeling guilty.

"I'm sorry, I had no idea," she explained plaintively to Kerry. "Don't worry though, we won't spend too much time with him if you don't want to."

"It's OK," laughed Kerry. "I've been dying to witness him in action. Now it looks like I'll..."

She stopped short, her face frozen in horror. "Oh, no!" she cried. "Sonja! Don't look round

now, but I've just seen Anna walk in. With Owen."

"What?! You're joking. Tell me you're having me on!" Seeing Kerry's horrified look, the colour drained dramatically from Sonja's face.

At that moment, Owen glanced over and saw Kerry. And the back of Sonja's head. He waved, said something to Anna, and they both came rushing over.

"Wow, what a coincidence!" they said in unison.

You're not wrong, thought Sonja ruefully.

"Yeah, we had no idea you were coming here," Sonja laughed (almost hysterically, in Kerry's opinion). "What a surprise!"

"Let me get you both a drink," Owen smiled, standing next to Sonja and looking so pleased to see her that she could have cut her tongue out right there and then.

"Thanks."

"And I must go to the loo," Anna said. "I won't be long."

They both went their separate ways and left Sonja in a state of panic. "What am I going to do?" she wailed. "How on earth am I going to get out of this?"

"Um, er... pass." Kerry replied, which only made Sonja more agitated.

"Come on, help me. I don't know what to do."

"Well, I uh, guess, um... we'll just have to keep them apart all night," Kerry finally spluttered in a flash of mild inspiration.

"Oh God, oh God, oh God! Here comes Kyle again. Quick, move over there."

Sonja hurriedly pushed Kerry into a dark recess of the club where Kyle followed them, carrying a round of drinks.

"Here you go, ladies," he smirked, handing out the glasses. "These should keep you going for a while."

Sonja caught sight of Owen walking past armed with drinks. He was obviously looking for them. She quickly turned her head away and squeezed herself behind a pillar.

"Something wrong, Son?" Kyle asked as she edged away from him.

"Er, no, it's just that light over your head, it's bothering my eyes a bit. Shall we all have a dance?" she added, noticing that Anna was loitering not far away and, although the place was heaving with people, could quite possibly spot them at any minute.

"Er... you girls go on ahead," said Kyle. "I'll sit this one out."

Sonja couldn't have moved any quicker if she'd sprouted wings. She dragged Kerry in the direction of the dance floor at the opposite end of the club

from Kyle, Owen and Anna. But instead of dancing, she pulled her friend into another dark corner.

"Can you see anyone?" she hissed.

"No, not at the moment. Oh, yes, I can see Kyle. He's talking to a big girl with pink hair. And... and... and Owen and Anna are coming this way."

Sonja gave a little moan before turning round to face them.

"We lost you," Owen said, then noticing the glasses in their hands, exclaimed, "Oh! You've already got drinks."

"We, uh, uh, we were thirsty. Managed to get served at this bar in double quick time," Sonja explained, nodding her head over to the bar in the corner. "Dance, anyone?"

Without waiting for a reply, but giving Kerry a look which said *Come with me. Now!* she headed for the dance floor. The others followed meekly. While they danced, Kerry and Sonja's radar tuned into possible sightings of Kyle. Fortunately, he was nowhere to be seen.

For the next couple of hours Sonja somehow managed to flit between the two guys, though she spent most of her time with Owen as Kyle seemed to be almost as elusive as she was. She was certain neither of them was aware of what was going on.

It was only when she and Kerry came back from the toilet to see Kyle and Owen standing with their backs to each other by one of the dance floors, that it all became too much for her. She grabbed Kerry by the arm and marched her in the opposite direction.

"We'll have to leave," she said definitely. "Right now. I'm sorry, Kez, but we'll have to go somewhere else. I can't take this any more."

"And how are you going to explain your disappearance next time you see the boys?" her sensible friend asked.

"Oh, I don't know. We'll say you were taken ill suddenly, and that I had to take you home. Something – *anything*. Please, Kez, can we just go before I get into any more trouble."

The girls hurried towards the exit and left.

• • •

"Remind me never ever, *ever* to get in such a mess again."

Sonja sat on the edge of her bed, put her head in her hands, and began rubbing her temples with her fingertips.

"I've got the most stinking headache imaginable," she wailed. "I must have aged twenty years, I'm a nervous wreck, and I've ruined your evening."

"Hey, come on," Kerry comforted her. "You haven't done that at all. I've had one of the most exciting nights of my life. It was like being in a scene from a sitcom."

"Oh, cheers," grumbled Sonja. "Here's me, barely surviving the worst time of my life, and all you can do is take the mick. I thought you were my friend, Kerry Bellamy!"

"Aw, come on," Kerry cajoled her, "lighten up! You'll be dining out on this one for years to come. And you have to admit, it was pretty funny. Or at least you will do one day."

"I can't imagine when," said Sonja morosely. "I don't know how people get away with this kind of thing. Some people manage to carry on behind their partners' backs for years. I can't even do it for a week!"

She looked up as another thought struck her.

"At least Cat wasn't there to see it, thank God!"

"You were pretty unlucky," Kerry said. "I know Winstead's not the most happening place on earth, but there are plenty of places to go on a Saturday night. The chances of you and the two guys you're seeing turning up at the same club on the same night must be pretty remote."

"Well, it's shown me I'm not cut out for this kind of thing," Sonja said. "Maya was right. I

would have been totally devastated if I'd been there and caught my boyfriend with someone else. I'll have to tell one of them I don't want to see him any more..."

She broke off and looked mournfully at Kerry. "But which one?"

CHAPTER 18

• •

THE TABLES ARE TURNED

Sonja picked up the phone and punched in Kyle's number. She knew it off by heart now, since she'd been trying to get him for most of the morning. So far, there had been no answer, which Sonja considered to be hugely inconvenient seeing as she was calling to dump him.

She had what she was going to say all planned out. About how she didn't think it was working out between them; how they didn't have very much in common; how she was studying for her A levels this year and didn't need any distractions; how they could still be friends...

Of course, all her reasons were merely excuses for the fact that she couldn't live a double life any more. And, much as she thought he was a great laugh and a bit of a challenge, Sonja couldn't

choose him over the divinely delicious Owen. *He* was something else.

Even though she knew she had a limited shelf-life with Anna's brother, Sonja thought he was worth it. When she went out with Kyle it was like dating a twelve-year-old; when she went out with Owen it was like going out with a really mature, thoughtful lad. There was no comparison and Sonja was prepared to swap Kyle for Owen, *if only he'd answer the phone*.

After twenty or so rings she gave up and then rang Anna's number at the flat. She needed to speak to Owen to apologise for Saturday night and hopefully (if he wasn't too angry about her running off from the club like that) to arrange to see him again.

No reply. Sonja slammed the phone back on its hook, grabbed her bag and left the house. She'd arranged to meet Matt in town and if she didn't hurry she'd be late.

Fortunately, she managed to catch a bus that was lumbering up the road near her house and it took her right to the Plaza. When she got to the mall café where they were meeting, she wasn't entirely surprised to see that Matt wasn't there yet.

Typical, she thought and wondered why she'd hurried in the first place. Matt was an even worse

timekeeper than she was, so she might have known he'd be late.

Sonja bought a cappuccino and sat at one of the tables overlooking the main part of the Plaza.It was the café where she'd sat with Kyle for the first time.

That seemed like an age ago, yet it was only a couple of weeks. Sonja sighed to herself as she thought of all that had gone on since then.

She looked up and scanned the mall for Matt. Where was he? He was getting on for twenty minutes late now – pretty poor even by Matt's lax standards.

Her gaze was drawn to a couple standing leaning against one of the display windows of the Body Shop. A girl with with long pink tresses had her back to Sonja and she was slowly entwining herself around the body of a guy who looked strangely... *familiar*.

Sonja leapt out of her seat and ran a few paces nearer for a closer look. Yes, it *was* him. Kyle – *her* Kyle! – and Pink Hair from the club on Saturday night were kissing and groping each other and giving it loads in the middle of the shopping centre.

Never one to think much about her actions before carrying them out, Sonja marched straight up to the couple and tapped Kyle on the shoulder.

Unsuckering his lips from Pink Hair's, he pulled away and opened his eyes. And found himself face to face with a seething Sonja.

"Well, *hello*. Fancy seeing you here!" she barked.

Kyle looked dumbfounded. Unlike Pink Hair who looked Sonja up and down and said, "Wos your problem?"

Then she looked at Kyle and added, "'Ere, Kyle-ey, who's she?"

Kyle-ey still couldn't engage his brain with his mouth. Instead, he looked from one to the other, a terrified expression on his face.

"Looks like you've been found out then," spat Sonja. "Are there any others I don't know about? The local hockey team perhaps?"

Pink Hair was becoming a bit agitated now. She obviously didn't have a clue what Kyle was up to.

A few passers-by had stopped to watch the free floor show, and this was bugging her even more – her eyes flitted from Sonja's to Kyle's to the smattering of shoppers having a gawp.

"Will one of you please tell me wos goin' on 'ere?" she squeaked, chewing on a piece of gum as if her life depended on it.

Kyle finally found his voice. "I uh, uh... I can explain," he said in little above a hoarse whisper,

his eyes darting from Sonja to Pink Hair and looking as though he might throw up at any minute.

"Is that really necessary?"

Although Sonja was beginning to see the funny side of the situation, she wasn't going to let Kyle off lightly. "I mean, why bother to open your mouth and say anything? I can guarantee that whatever comes out will be a pack of lies, so why waste the effort?"

Finally, the penny dropped for Pink Hair and she squared up furiously to Sonja. "'Ere, 'ave you been muckin' about with my Kyle-ey?" she demanded.

Sonja gave out a high-pitched cackle of derision.

"Mucking about with him? You must be joking!" she raged, shouting now. "But he's been mucking *me* about – and you too by the look of it. Anyway, I've finished with him now, so you're welcome to what's left. Though if you've got any self-respect you'll dump him too, the cheating rat!"

Sonja spun round and strode purposefully away, head held high, eyes blazing and a grin on her face a mile wide. Well, that was one way of getting her off the hook...

• • •

Owen had been in a bad mood ever since Sonja had disappeared from the club on Saturday night without saying goodbye. He wondered what she and Kerry had been up to – going off like that, without an explanation.

Now, sitting flicking through the Monday paper while Anna tried to clean the flat around him, he felt he had to do something before he exploded. He had been making excuses to pop downstairs to the café all morning, in the hope that Sonja might be there. But she wasn't and he didn't like to phone her because it made him sound desperate.

"I'm going for a walk," he announced suddenly, standing up abruptly and making Anna jump. "D'you want to come?"

Anna didn't hesitate. "No thanks. I must get this done – I don't often get the chance."

The truth was Anna was acutely aware of the mood her brother was in, and although she had done her best to reassure him that there must be a reasonable explanation for Sonja's vanishing act, it hadn't worked.

"I won't be long," he muttered as he left the flat. Anna smiled sympathetically and carried on cleaning. She had grown quite used to having her brother around.

Sure, he was a messy pig (but so were most guys) and he never told her when they were out

of milk or loo roll, but it was fun sharing her flat with him, even when he was in a grump.

Truly, if he decided to up sticks and move to Winstead, she'd be more than happy. In fact, she'd be over the moon. She bet Sonja would be too.

Aware that Ollie started his shift in the café soon, and keen to cheer Owen up, Anna decided to nip down to see if he could shed any light on Saturday night's events.

"Hi, Anna," he said brightly when she walked into the kitchen. "Did you have a good time on Saturday?"

"Yeah, fine. It was nice to get out and have a good dance. Actually, we bumped into Kerry and Sonja."

"I know, I heard," he smiled.

"You've spoken to Kerry then?" asked Anna hopefully. "Only they disappeared halfway through the evening. Didn't say goodbye or anything. I wondered if everything was all right. Did she say anything?"

Fortunately, Ollie had been prepared for this. And although he hated lying to anyone, Kerry had begged him so convincingly yesterday when she'd rung that he felt obliged to do so.

"Er, kind of," he said. "Kerry didn't feel too well so they decided to go home. Apparently, they looked everywhere for you, but couldn't see

you so they thought you must have left too. Obviously not."

"Oh, I see." Anna accepted the explanation without question. "No, we stayed until the small hours. Owen turned into a right misery guts once he realised Sonja had gone, but I had a good time. Anyway, I'll leave you to it – it looks like you've got quite a crowd out there."

Loaded down with burgers and chips and heading for the café, Ollie called 'Bye' over his shoulder and left the kitchen.

Anna rushed back up to her flat. She could hardly wait to tell Owen the good news. When she heard him rattling his key in the lock half an hour later, she flung the door open.

"Guess what?" she said gleefully, her eyes shining.

"Anna, please, I'm not in the mood," he replied in an exasperated voice. "If you've got something to tell me, just spit it out, will you?"

Anna told him of her conversation with Ollie and watched with delight as his expression changed from decidedly hangdog to thrilled surprise.

"Honest?" he said once she'd finished. "That's what really happened? So she wasn't avoiding me? That's brilliant, sis, I'm made up. I'll ring her straightaway."

As he went over to the phone, it began to ring.

"Go on, answer it," Anna said, smiling. "Maybe it's her."

Picking up the phone and pressing the receiver to his ear, Owen spoke.

"Hello?"

Anna wondered for a millisecond whether the call might – just might – be for her, but when she heard him say, "Yes, speaking", she realised it wasn't.

Suddenly, Owen's whole stance changed as he listened to the caller on the end of the line. His body became tense and his face took on a look of deep concentration.

Realising the call must be important, Anna earwigged Owen's half of the conversation. Not that she could gather much.

He was doing more of the listening rather than talking, saying "yes", and "really?" and "I had no idea" a lot and making Anna wish he'd get off the phone and tell her what was going on.

When, after about five minutes, he did put the receiver down, he turned to her, complete shock on his face, and said, "You won't believe what's just happened..."

CHAPTER 19

• •

BACK TO SQUARE ONE

As she made the short journey from her house to the End, Sonja wondered what was so important that Owen wanted to see her 'as soon as possible'.

When she had managed to catch him at home an hour ago, she had expected him to be peed off at the very least. *She* would be if the guy she was seeing had left a club without saying goodbye. But Owen sounded on top of the world.

She was only just coming to terms with the fact the Kyle had been two-timing her, probably for the entire time she had been seeing him. The irony was that he was obviously doing the same to her as she was to him on Saturday night with that nightmare with the pink hair.

No wonder he looked shocked – not delighted,

as Owen had been – to see her at the club. It explained why he wouldn't dance when she suggested it and why he seemed to be as evasive as she was.

And although she had laughed it off at the time, when she mulled over the scene of him with Pink Hair in the mall, she realised that her pride had been hurt, if nothing else. Imagine how she would feel if someone as nice as Owen had found out about her two-timing *him*. He'd be gutted.

At least Kyle was out of the picture now. It cleared the way for Sonja to concentrate on Owen for whatever time they had left.

Her thoughts returned to Owen and his insistence on seeing her so urgently.

Maybe he's decided to stay in Winstead? Wouldn't that be the best thing ever! she mused, her mood instantly lightening at the prospect. He could get a job locally, find a flat and they could get to know each other so much better. It would be brilliant.

Owen was perfect boyfriend material – mature, intelligent, amusing, nice and so damn gorgeous it hurt. Him staying would be the best thing that had ever happened to Sonja.

She was at the café now and she could see Owen from the window, sitting at the little corner table by the jukebox. She waved through the window and smiled as he waved back and stood

up, then came to meet her at the door as though he hadn't seen her for months.

"Sonja, great, come and sit down," he smiled, his pleasure at seeing her obvious. He took her by the arm and led her back to his table.

Sonja sat down and he asked her what she wanted to drink.

She watched him skip behind the counter to get the Diet Coke she'd requested.

Maybe Nick has offered him a job at the End? she mused. *Or in the record shop next door?* Nick was often short-staffed, so having Owen work alongside his sister would be an ideal solution for both of them. That would be even better: then Sonja could see him whenever she wanted, a bit like Kerry and Ollie.

Owen came back to the table with a couple of Cokes. "So, how are you?" he asked. "It feels like I haven't seen you for ages."

"Well, it's been nearly two days," Sonja laughed warmly at the compliment, "so, yeah, you're right, that is ages. I'm fine, really well."

"And how's Kerry?"

Sonja looked down at the table and felt guilt tinge her cheeks pink with embarrassment. "Oh, she's much better, thanks. She thinks she must have had a dodgy drink, that it made her feel a bit queasy. Anyway, how are you? You sounded pretty

upbeat on the phone. Have you won the Lottery or something?"

"Better than that," Owen beamed. "I've got a job."

Sonja could hardly contain herself. So she was right – he was staying. "That's great!" she beamed. "When do you start?"

"Tomorrow."

"Oh, fabulous! Will you be staying in Winstead then?" said Sonja excitedly.

"God, no," Owen replied. "It's nowhere round here. It's in Newcastle."

Sonja's mouth dropped. "*What?*"

"Newcastle," repeated Owen.

"Newcastle?" Sonja exclaimed in dismay. "I, uh, mean, what are you going to Newcastle for?"

"Oh, you wouldn't believe it, it's a great opportunity!" he enthused. "It's for a small firm working on the Internet. They were recruiting for new staff. I applied, though I didn't think I had a hope in hell of getting a job. I'm only a graduate after all.

"Anyway, I had an interview with them a month or so ago and because I hadn't heard anything, I'd forgotten all about it. But they've been trying to get in touch with me at home. In the end, they managed to speak to my flatmate and he gave them my number here. They've been trying to get hold of me but never managed to

catch anyone in. I only came off the phone to them just before you rang. They've offered me the job. Isn't that brilliant?"

Sonja could have cried. To have all her hopes dashed like this was the cruellest blow imaginable. But she couldn't let Owen know her true feelings, not now he was going. She turned her smile on full beam, leaned over the table and gave him a hug.

"That's wonderful news, Owen," she said. "The best. And I hope you'll be really happy there. You deserve it."

• • •

"Poor Son, what a rotten way for it all to end." Matt reached across and ruffled Sonja's hair affectionately with his hand.

Several days had gone by, Owen had left and Sonja's life was getting back to normal. So much so that as she sat in the End with her friends around her, a small part of her wondered if it had all been a giddy dream.

Sonja had gone from being a snog-free zone to hormonally hot stuff, in lust with not just one guy but two, and back to zilch again. Life was tough sometimes, she'd decided.

But it wasn't in Sonja's nature to be down for

long. She'd had a moan and a wail to Kerry, a moan to Matt, and now, as she recounted that final scene with Owen to the rest of the gang, she was just beginning to see the funny side.

"I mean," she guffawed, "there was I thinking that a university graduate and potential top web designer would be happy cleaning tables and serving up egg and chips in a greasy spoon! Just so we could be together. I must have had my brain on back to front."

"You're not going to go in for one of these long-distance love affairs then?" asked Cat.

Sonja shook her head. "I can't see the point. He might as well live in Timbuktu as Newcastle. He said I could go and stay anytime I like, but I can't see that happening. In a week or two he'll have forgotten all about me, and vice versa."

"That long?" Catrina frowned. "God, you must have it bad, girl."

"And I don't suppose Kyle is at the top of your entries in your Little Black Book, either," Matt chuckled. "*Get lost, you rat! Who are you after now, the whole hockey team?*" he mimicked, not for the first time since he'd heard about Sonja going full steam ahead in the mall.

"Not my best choice of boyfriend, I have to admit," conceded Sonja with a wry grin. "Though a good talking point for years to come, I think."

"But you haven't got anyone else up your sleeve, have you, Son?" Matt quizzed. "No one else you've got your sights set on?"

"Well, I'm always looking," she answered. "I'd like to think there might be someone else, and sooner rather than later. I think in the future though I'll stick to one at a time. It's less stressful that way."

She watched Matt laughing at what she'd said and thought how good-looking he was when he let rip with a natural laugh, rather than his contrived, look-at-me guffaw that sounded so false.

Matt could be quite good boyfriend material, she suddenly realised. He was funny and hunky, and she already knew him as a friend so she was aware of his bad points as well as the good.

She wondered if that was a thought worth pursuing...?

Sugar
SECRETS...
...& Mistakes

SNEAK PREVIEW!

"If you want to wait a while, I'll phone for a taxi," Matt offered. "I'll pay."

"No thanks, Mr Moneybags. You don't have to waste Daddy's allowance on me," trilled Cat, always quick to get a dig in at Matt and his cushioned lifestyle. "I'll just keep Joey company. And I fancy a walk."

She's up to something, thought Sonja, gazing at her cousin through narrowed eyes as she kissed Kerry goodnight and waved at the others.

Years of growing up with Cat and watching her get in and out of scrapes was qualification enough for Sonja to suss out when trouble was brewing. And apart from that, when was Cat – who never wore anything on her feet less than three inches high – *ever* in the mood to walk anywhere?

But this is Kerry's night, Sonja reasoned, *so I'm not going to spoil it by saying anything. Cat can't keep anything to herself for long, so we'll find out soon enough what she's up to...*

"Well, tonight's been great, Kerry – I've never actually had an Indian meal in an Indian restaurant before. I've only ever eaten it out of a foil tray when it's been delivered," admitted Matt, gazing round at the ornately papered walls and intricately decorated wall hangings of the restaurant.

"Really?" said Ollie in surprise, sitting up straight and pulling the small, wet towel off his face. While the girls had delicately wiped their fingers with the lemon-fragranced hot towels given to them by the waiter, Ollie had walloped his across his face with a groan of pleasure.

"You didn't say that when we came in." As often happened, Sonja was surprised that while Matt was one of the oldest and most 'privileged' (big house, posh boarding school, buckets of cash) of them all, he could be pretty naive too.

"Why give Cat *more* ammunition to have a go at me!" Matt shrugged good-naturedly.

"But you two *love* sniping at each other!" laughed Sonja.

"Oh, I don't think Matt loves it, do you, Matt? You've just got used to answering her back, haven't you?" Maya said intuitively.

"*She* always starts it. All I do is try and give back as good as I get."

"What is it – a bit of self-protection, then?" asked Anna, whose favourite hobby was working out what was going on inside people's heads. But she hadn't had anyone to practise her amateur psychology on since she'd moved to Winstead, until she'd started to hang out with Ollie and his friends.

"Whoa! It's like sitting in between Ricki Lake

and Oprah here!" Matt laughed, holding up his hands.

"Yes, but you haven't got as hard a shell as you pretend, have you, Matt?" smiled Maya.

"Me? I'm tough as anything!" he jokingly boasted, holding his arms out and flexing his muscles theatrically.

Maya reached over and tickled his armpit, and Matt crumpled up laughing.

"Hey, you know who you sounded like there!" said Ollie, reaching down into Kerry's bag.

"Furby!" the girls all squealed as Ollie placed the black and white furry toy – Matt's present to Kerry – on the table. He tickled its tummy and the creature burst into a mechanical rattle of giggles.

Looking over at Matt's grinning face, Sonja felt guilty at joining in with her cousin's teasing of him earlier in the evening. She was so used to Catrina and Matt's constant bickering that it hadn't really occurred to her that it might sometimes get a bit wearing for him.

So he's cocky and overconfident a lot of the time, but he's so sweet and kind too, she said to herself, thinking specifically of the goofy but perfect gift he'd chosen for Kerry. "I just saw it and thought it looked like Barney!" he'd explained when she unwrapped it. It was true – the fluffy toy did look like Kerry's lovable, daft dog.

In fact, Matt's a bit like Kyle and Owen rolled into one... Sonja mused.

Before her latest attempt at romance had fallen flat on its face, she'd been torn between Kyle's fun-loving but full-on character and Anna's sensitive and adorable brother, Owen. Neither of the relationships had come to anything; Owen had landed a job a long way away, while Kyle had shown his true colours by seeing someone else behind Sonja's back. Not that Sonja could complain about that, since she was guilty of doing exactly the same thing.

Yep, Sonja decided, *Matt certainly has Kyle's swagger and humour, but at least he's more reliable. And he's as handsome and can be as gentle as Owen, but doesn't live ten trillion miles away...*

Catching herself having these strange and unprecedented thoughts about her friend, Sonja experienced something that rarely happened to her – she blushed to the roots of her honey-blonde hair.

● ● ●

"Come on, there's one shot left – it's a shame to waste it," Maya cajoled the others later, as they stood shivering in their summer clothes in the cool evening air.

On her instructions, Ollie and Kerry snuggled up – with their backs to the window of the Kamil Tandoori restaurant and the glances of the curious waiters inside – while Anna stood to their left, and Sonja and Matt posed to their right.

"Son – budge up to Matt! I can't get you all in!" Maya waved over at them, her face obscured by the camera.

"C'mere, you!" said Matt, boisterously pulling Sonja in close to him.

The heat from his body so close to hers burned through Sonja's thin cotton dress.

"Matt!" barked Maya, dropping her camera down. "What on earth have you got stuck to your lip? Is it a bit of nan bread you were saving for later?"

"Huh? Where? Son – check it out for me!" said Matt, turning to Sonja.

With one finger, Sonja reached up and brushed the bit of bread away from his lips, wondering for a fleeting moment what it would be like to kiss them...

DO YOU ACT BEFORE YOU THINK?

• •

Cat's obviously got something up her sleeve at the moment, but Sonja's definitely got stuff on her mind too! The question is, will their actions come from their hearts or their heads?

Are you the kind of girl that always thinks things through, or do you go with your first instinct and consider the consequences later? Look at the following scenarios and think about how you'd react if they happened to you.

---

1.   Would you describe yourself as...

a)   Cautious – although sometimes you wish you were braver?

b)   Someone who takes chances – even if they sometimes don't work out?

---

2.   When you've got to make a decision, do you...

a)   Think about all the pros and cons before you make your mind up?

b)   Go with your first, gut reaction (and keep your fingers crossed behind your back)?

3. Out of the blue, you decide to get your eyebrow pierced/get a pet rat/chuck in school. Would you...

a) Talk it over with your mates or your parents before you went ahead?

b) Act on your instincts and surprise them all?

4. You spill a secret ambition or plan in front of a few mates. If their reaction is a big thumbs-down, would that make you...

a) Stop and think for a bit, before you do anything drastic?

b) All the more determined to do it?

5. You decide to do something – like take a course – that none of your friends are involved in. You feel nervous about going it alone, but...

a) Confident too – after all, you've given it a lot of thought.

b) Excited – the thrill of the unknown makes it even more challenging.

6. You're hanging out with one particular mate and having a great laugh. Thing is, he's a lad. Does it ever cross your mind that he'd make a great boyfriend?

a) Yes, but you wouldn't rush anything. Why ruin a beautiful friendship?

b) Yes! It's obviously destiny!

7. You've done something you know your parents are going to flip out over. Do you...

a) Bite the bullet and tell them calmly, hoping to get it over with as soon as you can?

b) Put off telling them for as long as possible?

8. Your parents find out what you've done and hit the roof. Do you...

a) Try to see it their way, and do your best to have good answers for the questions they're going to throw at you?

b) Lose it completely and tell them they've forgotten what it's like to be young?

9. Do you believe in fate?

a) Maybe, but a little bit of luck and a lot of good sense have more to do with getting what you want.

b) Yes, and that's why you've got to follow your heart when it comes to big decisions.

10. Cupid's arrow is...

a) Like love at first sight. You feel it all right, but you still want to get to know someone properly before you give your heart away.

b) What life's all about. You can't argue when that thunderbolt of love strikes you!

NOW CHECK OUT HOW YOU SCORED...

SCORES

● ●

An equal mixture of a and b

There are times when you use reason to work out what to do (something Cat never does!); at other times you go with your feelings. That's a good balance: you know the importance of thinking things through, as well as being able to tune into your instincts. Learning to use both your senses – your common sense and your intuition – means any decision you come to will probably be the right one.

Mostly a

You live by logic, looking at a situation inside, outside and every which side before you make a decision. It's a pretty sensible approach, but occasionally, the more you analyse something, the more you can get in a muddle about it. That's when you need to take a leaf out of Cat's book and go with the vibes you're getting, rather than just trusting the bare facts.

Mostly b

Your heart rules your head, and while that's romantic and exciting, it can also land you in a whole lot of trouble! Like Cat, you leap into things on a whim, and while things could work out OK, you might just end up regretting not listening to that little voice in your head. Nobody's saying you've got to give up trusting your instincts, it's just that you should also check in with what your noddle's got to say before you dive in!

Sugar
SECRETS...
...& Revenge

LOVE!
Cat's in love with the oh-so-gorgeous
Matt and don't her friends know it.

HUMILIATION!
Then he's caught snogging Someone
Else at Ollie's party.

REVENGE!
Watch out Matt – Cat's claws are out...

Meet the whole crowd in the first ever
episode of Sugar Secrets.

*Some secrets are just too good to
keep to yourself!*

Collins
An imprint of HarperCollinsPublishers
www.fireandwater.com

Sugar
SECRETS...
...& Rivals

FRIENDS!
Kerry can count on Sonja – they've been best friends forever.

BETRAYAL!
Then Ollie's sister turns up and things just aren't the same.

RIVALS!
How can Kerry possibly hope to compete with the glamorous Natasha?

Some secrets are just too good to keep to yourself!

Collins
An imprint of HarperCollins*Publishers*
www.fireandwater.com

Sugar
SECRETS...

...& Lies

CONFESSIONS!
Is Ollie in love? Yes? No? Definitely maybe!

THE TRUTH!
Sonja is determined to find out who the lucky girl can be.

LIES!
But someone's not being honest, which might just break Kerry's heart...

Some secrets are just too good to keep to yourself!

Collins

An imprint of HarperCollins*Publishers*
www.fireandwater.com

Sugar
SECRETS...
...& Freedom

FAMILIES!
They can drive you insane, and Maya's at breaking point with hers.

GUILT!
There's tragedy in store – but is Joe partly to blame?

FREEDOM!
The price is high, so who's going to pay...?

Some secrets are just too good to keep to yourself!

Collins
An imprint of HarperCollinsPublishers
www.fireandwater.com

Coming in November 1999

Sugar
SECRETS...
...& Ambition

GIRLS!
Matt's surrounded by them – but why
are they making him so nervous?

TENSION!
An unexpected party guest stirs up old
resentments and sets Sonja thinking
about her future.

AMBITION!
Sonja's aiming for The Top, but will she
have any friends left when she gets there?

*Some secrets are just too good to
keep to yourself!*

Collins
An imprint of HarperCollins*Publishers*
www.fireandwater.com

Order Form

To order direct from the publishers, just make a list of the titles you want and fill in the form below:

Name ....

Address ....

....

....

Send to: Dept 6, HarperCollins Publishers Ltd, Westerhill Road, Bishopbriggs, Glasgow G64 2QT.

Please enclose a cheque or postal order to the value of the cover price, plus:

UK & BFPO: Add £1.00 for the first book, and 25p per copy for each additional book ordered.

Overseas and Eire: Add £2.95 service charge. Books will be sent by surface mail but quotes for airmail despatch will be given on request.

A 24-hour telephone ordering service is available to Visa and Access card holders: 0141- 772 2281

Collins
An *Imprint* of HarperCollins*Publishers*

ALSO BY HA JIN

Fiction

Poetry

THE BRIDEGROOM

Ha Jin was born in 1956 in Liaoning, China and spent six years serving in the People's Liberation Army. He left China in 1985 for the United States, where he earned a PhD at Brandeis University. He is the author of two books of poetry; three collections of stories, *Under the Red Flag*, which won the Flannery O'Connor Award for Short Fiction in 1996, *Oceans of Words*, which won the PEN/Hemingway Award in 1997 and *The Bridegroom*; and two novels, *In the Pond* and *Waiting*, winner of the 1999 National Book Award for Fiction, and the 2000 PEN/Faulkner Award. Ha Jin lives near Atlanta, Georgia, where he is a professor of English at Emory University.